Hauling Checks
Alex Stone

AWS Books
Columbus, Ohio

Alex Stone

AWS BOOKS, November 2009

ISBN 1449563333
EAN-13 9781449563332

rev date: 01/2019

cannondle@aol.com
www.haulingchecks.com

Printed in the United States of America

This book is dedicated to all the Freight Dogs who are out there every night hauling the work to any place, at any time, in any weather.

Alex Stone

Freight Dog -

A pilot that flies an under-automated aircraft in dismal weather conditions, is never late, and is a much better pilot than you are.

- UrbanDictionary.com

Alex Stone

<u>Chapter Index</u>

Hauling Checks

Alex Stone

Author's Note:

This is a work of fiction. The pilots and other employees of the air cargo industry are actually nothing like the characters in this novel. They are extremely professional people who have a very high regard for safety.

Alex Stone

- 1 -
Introduction

I'm a cargo pilot. In the industry, I'm known as a "Freight Dog." I fly canceled checks and other types of high-value cargo around the country, mostly at night, in airplanes that are older than I am. Flying freight—or "work" as we call it—in small, twin-engine aircraft is a lesser known side of the aviation world. Our day starts when banker's hours end. Thousands of flights move millions of pounds of work from city to city every night while the rest of the country is asleep. If you consider flying to be a sport (if you've flown with us you would), then this sport would fall into a similar category as bull riding. It's rough, and it's a non-stop spree of broken airplanes, bad weather, sketchy characters, and everything-went-wrong situations.

We live by the motto "Any place, Any time, Any weather." We work in difficult conditions trying to maintain strict deadlines for our customers, who are mostly the nation's largest banks. We're out there in the freezing rain getting de-iced when you're laying down for bed. We're sweeping the snow off our wings with a broom at three in the morning. That horrible thunderstorm you heard last night while you were sleeping, we were flying through it. The fog you woke up to in the early morning hours, we were landing in it.

Freight dogs get their nickname from their get-out-there-and-get dirty attitude. We often load and unload our own airplanes in the summer heat, rain, or winter snow. Then we jump behind the controls, still soaking wet from the rain or with frozen fingers from the cold for an immediate departure.

Our antique airplanes aren't as pretty as the passenger planes most people are accustomed to seeing. They never get washed, rarely get new paint jobs, and often look like they just flew through a sandstorm. The paint is chipping off in sheets, primer has been sprayed on to protect the bare metal, and bent parts are either bent back or patched over. The cockpit trim is usually beat up and broken, pieces that have fallen off have been replaced with sheet metal, door handles have been replaced with ropes, seat springs are blown out, and the floor is plywood. Everything aft of the cockpit has been hollowed out, or "canned out" as we call it, because the interior resembles the inside of a soda can.

The average cargo plane has four times the amount of time on the airframe over the average passenger plane. Our planes don't have the modern glass panel displays; we have primitive "steam-gauge" instrumentation and the most cutting-edge nineteen-seventies' technology avionics.

Just like our airplanes, cargo pilots don't have the same look of our passenger counterparts. We don't wear the spiffy uniforms with the epaulets and tie—what we call "monkey suits"—that the passenger airline pilots wear. Cargo pilots have been described as looking homeless. You'll often find us catching a nap in the dark corners of the airport in between flights at odd hours of the night. We wear t-shirts, shorts, and flip-flops in the summer, and sweatshirts, jeans and tennis shoes in the winter. We are not required to shave or look in any way "presentable."

The movement of checks and other financial documents has been the backbone of our industry for decades. However, in recent years, the decline in the use of paper checks and the implementation of electronic check transfer has threatened our business. Our industry is becoming obsolete, and, before long, Freight Dogs may be a thing of the past. Check hauling companies have been dropping like flies, and I'm starting to fear we might be next.

Alex Stone

Part One:
Fly the Unfriendly Skies

Alex Stone

- 2 -
The Ride of Shame

Riding the tug to the ramp that's towing your disabled airplane off the runway is always an embarrassing situation. What do I say to the line guy who's driving the tug that's towing my crippled airplane? It's a long, slow ride across the airport; gotta say something. "These seats are pretty comfortable," I said. That's the best I could come up with.

The line guy mustered little response to my failed attempt at conversation. "Yup," was all he said. Behind us, my worthless copilot was riding in the plane. At the moment I was a little jealous of him. *I should have stayed in the plane,* I thought. Now I've got to make small talk with the tug driver. "What's the biggest plane you've ever pulled with this thing?" I asked.

"Huh?" He didn't hear me over the deafening roar from the jet taking off on the runway parallel to us.

"Never mind," I mumbled.

I peered back over my shoulder at the dingy, faded brown Navajo Cheiftain that dragged behind us. The bright sunshine that morning highlighted the red fiberglass that had been slapped on the front of the engine cowlings in a crude attempt to hold them together, while an ever-increasing number of cracks threatened to break them apart. It looked like a corpse of an airplane that should be parked in a Mojave Desert Aircraft Graveyard. I rarely flew during daylight hours, and seeing one of our planes in the sunlight reminded me of just how old and decrepit they really were. Cargo planes are better suited to night time flying, where their innumerable flaws were hidden by the cover of darkness.

Others were taking notice of the sad state of my plane as well. We crossed an intersection in the taxiway; passing in front of a shiny new Gulfstream V. I could see the pilots staring at my Navajo as they waited for us to pass. Their faces displayed a look of pity for whoever had to fly that thing.

How I found myself in this embarrassing situation involved a terrible nose wheel vibration, encountered during takeoff from Dallas Love Field about an hour ago. You would think an extreme vibration on the takeoff roll would call for an aborted takeoff. Nah, why not go with it and see what happens? And I told myself, "I'll figure it out in the air."

During the takeoff roll, my copilot, who's known as The Co, was completely useless as usual. He was still sleeping off his hangover from the night before, and the most help he could offer me as I struggled to get the crippled airplane off the ground was mumbling, "What the hell are you doing? Keep the noise down; I'm trying to sleep!"

The Co and I are Freight Dogs.

Known to be some of the best and toughest pilots out there, most people would take great pride in calling them self a Freight Dog, but not me. That's because I work for an airline called Checkflight.

Based out of a rural town in Ohio, Checkflight is a small mom-

and-pop type freight outfit that specializes in hauling checks. And In the business of hauling checks, Checkflight is the worst. It hasn't always been that way, though. Not all that long ago, there was a time when this was a respectable company to fly for. In fact, a few years ago when I was hired business was booming, we had a great group of pilots, and I actually enjoyed working here. But, as times got tough, things around here went downhill quickly. In order to stay in business, management had to "cut costs;" basically, they cut everything. We are now understaffed, underpaid, and underequipped to do the job.

Over the past couple years; things at Checkflight have gotten more and more dysfunctional by the day. Most of the first-rate freight dogs this company used to employ, were either "let go," or became so fed up with the state of things around here that they left on their own accord; some have even decided to quit aviation altogether. But, as for me; I'm still here.

For the past year I have been looking for another job. The problem is, these days the whole aviation industry is slipping into the toilet. There are more unemployed pilots out there than ever before, no one is hiring, and due to Checkflight's rapidly deteriorating reputation, having them on my resume sure isn't aiding in my search for employment elsewhere.

I just hope I make it out of here alive before this ship sinks.

Cutting corners on maintenance has become a standard practice at Checkflight. We now only have one mechanic; his name is Tony. Tony's departmental budget has been cut to zero. Fixing things properly is a last resort. His primary job is to convince the pilots that the plane is not actually broken, we "just don't know how to operate it properly." He often offers advice to solve mechanical issues, such as, "hit it with a hammer," "try it again and see what happens," or "I wouldn't worry about that."

Since the planes we fly almost always have some sort of mechanical issue prior to taking off, it's led the pilots to adopt the phrase "I'll figure it out in the air." Meaning take off first, then try to figure out what the problem is once you're airborne. If you spend too much time sitting on the ground trying to problem solve, you're gonna be late, and in this business on time performance meant everything.

"I'll figure it out in the air"—this same phrase had been used on a previous occasion prior to departing with a fuel fire in the right engine. I had noticed unusually high temperatures on the gauges while holding short of the runway waiting to take off, but I decided to depart anyway. After getting airborne, the engine became engulfed in flames. I was unable to get the fire extinguished, which resulted in a return to the airport. Not an emergency landing, just "gotta go back to the ramp." At least, that's what I told air traffic control because declaring an emergency involves paperwork.

"Checkflight 101, are you sure you don't need any assistance?" the control tower had asked me. It was obvious that he could see the flames, but I wasn't going to admit to any sort of problem.

"Nope, we're good," I responded. I took a quick glance at the fuel fed inferno on our right wing, and repeated again "Just gotta go back to the ramp." If I just say I have to go back to the ramp and leave it at that, the plane would still technically be airworthy. If I told air traffic control what was really going on, that I had a pretty serious problem, I would have to write up the airplane. The plane would be grounded until it was fixed properly, and if I grounded an airplane just because the engine caught on fire, my boss (The Chief) would be pissed.

The Chief is both the owner and the Chief Pilot of Checkflight, and he doesn't like it when planes are grounded. A plane sitting on the ground equals lost revenue. His motto is, "If it's not falling out of the sky, then it should be flying." We weren't falling out of the sky yet, just burning a little, so, "Extinguish the fire, put some duct tape on that broken fuel hose, and you should be good to go." The Chief had said when we pulled back onto the ramp; and that's just what we did. Minutes later our now slightly charred airplane was rolling down the runway again, departing into the nighttime sky.

Back to the current problem at hand; this vibration issue.

Taxing to the runway in Dallas something seemed out of sorts with the way the plane was handling. There was a definite lack of shock absorption in the nose gear and a mushiness in turns. This in itself wasn't much cause for alarm though as many of our airplanes handle poorly on the ground, most likely the result of several off-runway excursions in their past. But, upon beginning the takeoff roll, it became apparent that something was definitely wrong, or at least more wrong than normal anyway.

It's hard to remember a flight where I would describe things as being "right." Abnormal was the norm— so I went with it.

The old Navajo shuddered as I released the brakes. Naturally, I did the only logical thing and continued with the takeoff. Holding the throttles firewalled, the engines surged over redline. The plane shook with increasing violence as it gained speed due to the yet unknown source of vibration. This was in addition to the usual left to right yawing as the prop RPM varied plus-or-minus three-hundred; the prop governors failing to maintain a constant speed*.

*- This is the prop governors job; maintaining constant speed. The prop governors use oil pressure to adjust the pitch of the propeller blades to maintain a constant speed (prop RPM) set by the pilot; hence the name "Constant Speed Prop". But, like everything in our airplanes, they don't work properly. The speed varies wildly, the left and right engines run unevenly, and the plane swerves back and forth.

The further into the takeoff roll we got, maintaining control of the aircraft became more and more difficult. Even though we were still not fast enough to become airborne, I became increasingly concerned over how much longer this thing would hold together. While most airlines instruct their pilots to make responsible go or no-go decisions, this situation would most definitely fall into the no-go category, at Checkflight, the answer is always GO!

Gotta get this thing off the runway, I thought, and I pulled back on the control yoke, which brought the weight off of the nose wheel, lifting it off the ground. The vibration stopped. Satisfied that the problem was solved, I continued to lift the main wheels off of the ground. But the plane wasn't ready to fly. For a few moments we hung there, just a few feet above the runway, with the wings gasping for airspeed. I retracted the landing gear, cutting our drag. Slowly the airspeed crept upwards, and we climbed away from the runway.

Upon becoming airborne my mind began replaying the events that just took place. *What the hell was that?* I thought. Having difficulty maintaining directional control on the runway was an everyday occurrence in these old airplanes, but that was ridiculous.

Several minutes passed before I realized that the radios seemed quiet. This was a little odd, especially since we were at a busy airport. Normally after takeoff the control tower would be handing us off to departure control, but all I could hear in my headset was The Co snoring. That's when I realized the vibration had shaken my communications radio right out of the instrument panel. I should note that it's my copilot's job to man the radios, but he's over there drooling on his hoodie. Once again, I was stuck here dealing with these problems all by myself.

After reseating the radio, it was needless to say Love Tower was a little upset with our lack of response to numerous radio calls. "Checkflight 101, how do you hear Love Tower!?" I heard him screaming as the radios came back to life.

"We're here," I said into my mic, "just had a little radio problem."

"I've been trying to call you for several minutes!" The controller shouted back.

"Sorry," I apologized, "we just had a little problem with the radios. Everything's fine now."

"Alright 101, contact departure."

"Checkflight 101 is calling departure."

Cleared to land in Austin, The Co is now awake. For him, it's time to do the real work—going to the hotel bar. He was getting ready by attempting to smooth out his bed-head as I made our final approach.

"Gear down." I called out. This was The Co's queue to be of some use and move the gear handle, but he just stared at me in bewilderment.

"Oh, sorry, almost forgot who I was flying with. Here let me get that myself." I said as I moved the gear handle down. I'd been flying with The Co long enough to know that he wasn't going to do it, but I keep humoring myself in the hopes that one day he will actually become a contributing member of this crew.

Two-hundred feet. "Full flaps——Never mind I got it" I laughed while moving the flap handle.

We touched the main wheels down on runway two-eight-right; so far, a smooth landing, then I set the nose wheel down. The plane started to shimmy and shake like the wheels were going to fall off.

This airplane was not exactly what I would call "a solid machine" to start with, so all this shaking can't be good. I had a momentary vision of every nut and bolt on the airplane vibrating loose, and the whole plane falling apart right there on the runway. I pictured The Co and me just sitting in the middle of the runway, in a pile of aircraft parts, wondering what the hell happened.

It didn't take me long to realize that the vibration we had encountered on the takeoff roll was back. Just then, out of the corner of my eye, I saw a chunk of rubber being thrown from the left side of the nose. *There goes the tire.*

I Stood on the brakes. Sparks flew as the bare rim ground into the pavement. All the while, The Co just bitched about the air conditioning not working. "I can't believe they still haven't fixed the a/c in this thing," he complained, "It's fucking hot. Open the vents."

"I'm a little busy right now." I said, "Open them yourself." But, The Co just sat there with his arms crossed, he wasn't about to do anything for himself.

I managed to get the plane stopped without running off into the grass. Now for the embarrassing part. "Austin Tower, this is Checkflight 101, we've got a flat tire, we're gonna need a tug," I said into the mic. I was sure that The Chief would disagree with my decision to call a tug, but there were way too many people around here at this time of day to taxi across the airport on a bare rim. Somebody would notice, so I was forced to do the right thing.

"Roger that Checkflight 101; I'll send a tug out there…break…ATTENTION all aircraft this is Austin Tower: we have a disabled aircraft on the runway. The airport is temporarily closed," the controller announced for all to hear.

And that's how I ended up on the tug, taking the ride of shame.

Upon arriving on the ramp, the courier who would be delivering our work to the bank was waiting for us in his dilapidated cargo van. He looked like someone who wasn't allowed within three-hundred yards of a school, and his rape van definitely wasn't helping his creepy image. On the weekends, he probably used that van to lure children away from playgrounds with promises of bicycles and candy.

Having to wait for the tug had caused us to miss our arrival time, and the courier wasn't very happy about us being late. Bank deadlines were tight; any delay usually meant missing them.

I helped the courier unload the plane of the fifteen hundred pounds of work, with no help from The Co of course, as he had conveniently gone missing. I threw the boxes and bags of checks out the back of the plane onto the ramp. The courier picked them up, tossing them into his van, all the while he went on and on bitching about how fast, and recklessly, he was going to have to drive in order to make it to the bank on time. "Do you know what traffic downtown is like at this time of the day?" he asked. "I'm gonna have to do ninety on the shoulder if I'm gonna make these deadlines."

"Wow dude, that sucks." I said, sarcastically.

"Why were you late anyway?"

"Our tire blew. We had to get a tow. Shit happens."

"Well, if I was flying that thing I would be on time."

"Oh, you would? Do you know how to fly?" I got no response. "So, you don't know what you're talking about?" Still no response.

When the last box was in his rape van, the courier jumped in and shut the doors from the inside. Moments later, a puff of black smoke shot out of the tail pipe when he hotwired the starter. I stood there for a minute, watching him tear off across the ramp with little regard for the people running to get out of his way.

I called maintenance and spoke with Tony about our busted-up airplane. He was less than pleased that we had reported the incident to the control tower; this meant that the tire would actually have to be fixed. "You couldn't have kept your mouth shut till you got the plane back home?" he asked me.

"No," I said, "the plane was shaking out of control, and the tire completely shredded off the rim. What did you want me to do, fly home on a bare rim?"

"Yes!" Tony said, "That is exactly what you should have done. Now I'm gonna have to beg The Chief for the money to pay for this."

"Well, it's gotta be fixed," I told him, "so, do what you've gotta do."

Any money spent on maintenance had to be cleared through The Chief, and any amount greater than zero was too expensive. Since we were away from our home base, Tony would have to contract the repair to an outside source, meaning it would cost even more. On top of that, they didn't have the right size tire here in Austin, so Tony would have to ship a tire out here on another flight, further adding to the cost for the repair.

It was questionable at best whether or not this thing would actually be fixed in time for our return flight tomorrow. Judging by what usually happens, Tony would no doubt send the wrong parts and the mechanics here in Austin would probably just have to resort to some sort of last-minute patch job.

Even on an unlimited budget, I had my doubts about Tony's ability to keep these planes in working order. The only showcase of his mechanical abilities, that I'd seen, was his primer grey eighty-six

Camaro, that he was constantly working on, yet it never seemed to run properly. I'm not even sure that he was an aircraft mechanic in the first place, or any kind of mechanic, for that matter.

The Chief had hired Tony straight out of prison, through some program that gave tax cuts to employers who help reintegrate former inmates back into society. Upon The Chief's request, Tony still wore his orange prison jumpsuit to work. I think The Chief felt that having an ex-convict as a mechanic would deter the pilots from reporting any mechanical discrepancies, because of this, Tony would never really have to fix anything, making it unnecessary for him to have any kind of real mechanical knowledge.

"You know I should shank you for this." Tony said, obviously getting frustrated with me.

"I don't think a shanking is necessary Tony," I said, "just send a tire, please."

"Fine, I'll see what I can do. Go ahead and write the airplane up."

So, I wrote up the squawk in the aircraft maintenance log: *Airplane don't work right on runway.* Nobody takes these things seriously anyway.

The last thing to do before leaving the airport was checking out with dispatch. I hated calling dispatch. The two dispatchers we had were both crazy. One of them is a senile old woman named Barbara who always talks about her bowel movements, or the lack thereof when she's constipated.

Barbara is ninety-two and has been with the company for thirty-seven years. She works for next to nothing, because she hasn't asked for a raise since nineteen eighty-two, so The Chief won't let her go even though she suffers from dementia and is usually confused about what day it is.

Barbara happily comes to work every morning wearing a matching sweat suit, a different color every day, of course, and spends most of her day playing bingo on her computer.

The other dispatcher is Karen. She's in her twenties, though you wouldn't know it from looking at her. She looks twice her age; time having not been good to her.

Karen claims that she recently got married, but no one has ever seen her new husband. Most of us think she's making him up. She is always telling stories about him that just don't add up. Just the other day, she told me that her husband was being deployed to Iraq, but, when he got to the airport for the deployment flight, the plane wouldn't start. So naturally, the Army just sent him home and said "We'll catch you next time." I found that a little hard to believe, which is why I questioned whether or not he even exists in the first place.

Karen is just as gullible as she is a bull shitter. The Chief hired her because he was able to convince her that the new minimum wage in Ohio was three dollars an hour. She bought it, and it got us one of the worst dispatchers in the business.

The phone rang twice, then I heard, "Dispatch. This is Barbara."

"Hi Barbara, it's 101 checking out."

"Okay," she said, "I'll check you out, but have you considered that offer I made for your dog?"

"What dog, Barbara?" I asked. "I don't have a dog."

"I have offered you forty dollars for that dog," she shrieked. "I feel that's a reasonable offer."

"I don't know what you're talking about Barbara! Will you just check us out please?"

"Okay, I'll check you out. Who is this again?"

"It's 101"

"Okay, 101 checked out. Now go out that door and get on the ferry to the Bronx."

"What's that?" I questioned. I heard her but…

"Go out that door and get on the ferry to the Bronx." She repeated.

"Uhh…Okay, we'll do that, thanks Barbara." Sometimes you just have to play along.

After checking out with dispatch, we were off to the hotel. Check in at the hotel was a problem because our company forgot to make a reservation. Barbara was in charge of making hotel reservations, and she often forgets, but, after some angry noise about whether or not our credit was valid, we had our rooms.

"You gonna sleep at all?" I asked The Co as he walked into his room.

"Hell no! I'm going to the pool bar!" He shot back. Exactly what I expected him to say.

"I'll meet you there," I said.

So, there I was the next morning pounding on The Co's hotel room door. "We're late!" I yelled. "Open the door, you ass!"

After five minutes of pounding, the door finally swung open, and there was The Co standing there in the same clothes he had been wearing the night before; he was soaking wet, and looked like death.

"Good, you're alive," I said, "we gotta go; we're late and the hotel wants us out now … and why are you wet?"

"Oh, I slept on the balcony," he tells me like it was no big deal.

"You slept on the balcony, but it's been storming?"

"Yea, I didn't notice till just now," he said, shaking water out of his hair. "I sort of fell asleep out there."

"Sort of?" I questioned. Then I remembered the events of the last 24 hours, and this no longer surprised me.

By the time I got down to the pool yesterday, The Co was already completely shit canned. There he was slamming a bottle of tequila at the pool bar. It looked like he was already half way through the bottle, and we had only been at the hotel for thirty minutes. I decided that I wanted no part of that, so I went to the restaurant to grab something to eat.

It must have been about the time my food arrived that The Co was being fished out of the pool by hotel security.

Now, I didn't see it, but the people who did claimed he was floating in the pool like a buoy, completely blacked out. It took two security guards to drag him out and strap him into a wheel chair.

Hotel security approached me in the restaurant and asked, "Was that your friend in the red shorts at the pool bar?"

I knew the correct answer was yes, but I hesitated, not sure if I wanted to involve myself in whatever The Co had done.

"Yes, I know him," I responded cautiously.

"We just had to drag him out of the pool. He was unconscious," said one of the security guards.

Here we go again I thought as I got up to follow them, leaving my lunch behind.

When we entered the lobby, there was The Co strapped into a wheel chair that was parked in the corner. Kids were walking by, pointing, "Mommy what's wrong with that man?"

As I walked up, a man in a suit, who was waiting next to the wheel chair, identified himself as the hotel manager and asked me to help wheel The Co up to his room.

"Sure," I said fighting back the urge to laugh.

The elevator door closed, and I hit the button for the third floor. Then I took one look at The Co all slumped over, mumbling barely audibly, and I lost it. I covered my mouth, turning my head towards the corner, trying to hide my laugh. I tried to make small talk with the manager, who was obviously disappointed with the situation, in an attempt to lighten the mood a little.

I looked around the elevator, trying to think of something to say. "Otis," I said, "This elevator's an Otis, good elevator." Laughing even harder, I noticed the weight restriction on the elevator plaque. "This thing's got a takeoff weight of forty-five hundred pounds," I said.

"This is a very serious situation, sir," the manager said sternly. "This is a family establishment, and we don't like your kind."

Hotels are always prejudiced against cargo pilots, I wonder why? It's hard to blame them when people like The Co give us such a good reputation.

I realized that I had to be serious for a few minutes or we'd have to find another hotel for the night. I was in no mood for that, and, judging by The Co's condition, I doubt that he was either.

Even at a spring break bash, The Co's behavior would be considered borderline unacceptable. At a family hotel on a weekday, he was completely out of line.

I decided to just keep my mouth shut, and as I stood there in the uncomfortable silence, I was reminded of some of The Co's other public displays of questionable behavior.

I thought of the time, when on a previous overnight trip, I had suggested that we eat dinner at the Japanese steakhouse that was next to our hotel.

Upon walking into the restaurant, The Co had asked me, "Do they have Keystone at this place?"

"I'm not sure," I'd said. "Probably not."

"Well, if they don't have Keystone here, I'm fucking leaving!" He'd said loud enough for everyone around us to hear.

The Co doesn't exactly have a filter on his mouth.

Then, when we were seated and asked to remove our shoes, The Co protested. I had to calm him down and insist that he take his shoes off or they weren't going to serve us.

"I'm hungry, so you better not ruin this!" I'd told him.

After several minutes of arguing, finally he complied and removed his shoes. Instantly it became very clear why he didn't want to in the first place. His socks were covered in paint, full of holes, and they stunk. "Oh my god, put your shoes back on!" I'd said disappointed and embarrassed, and told him, "Let's go!"

We ended up finding a bar to eat at that suited The Co's sophisticated taste and served Keystone.

There was also the time we went to an all you can eat seafood buffet in Indianapolis. Where we were asked to leave after The Co tried to discreetly puke under our table in his attempt to "make room for more."

Maybe, this hotel manager would feel better if I pointed out the fact that; at least The Co hadn't puked in his pool. Doubt it.

We got The Co into his room and dumped him in his bathtub.

Before leaving, the manager warned me that one more disturbance from us and he would have us removed from the premises. I decided we needed to lay low for a while till the heat was off, so I spent the rest of the afternoon watching Cash Cab in my hotel room.

About three hours later, there was a knock at the door. I opened it to find The Co standing there with a green bottle, a spoon, and a handful of sugar packets. "What the hell is this?" I asked.

"Absinthe," he said. "It's what Van Gogh was drinking when he cut his ear off."

"Where'd you get it?"

"Mexico. I brought it with; thought we might get bored."

"Why would you want to drink it if it's going make you cut your ear off?"

"I'm not going to cut my ear off. I'm just going to trip balls."

Great.

"You want some?"

"No, I'm good; but when did you go to Mexico?"

"Oh, one of the other pilots and me borrowed a plane and went down there a few weeks ago."

"What do you mean *borrowed?* Actually, never mind. I don't want to know."

The Co set up a make-shift chemistry lab which he used to mix several shots of the green alcohol, by pouring it over spoonfuls of sugar. He slammed back one after another; he then dumped a few sugar packets into a flask, followed by the remainder of the absinthe. "You ready to go out?" He asked.

"We're going out?"

"Yes." The Co answered me like I'd just asked the stupidest question he'd ever heard.

"Ahh, alright," I said.

"Let's go!" He said, and before I could even get my shoes on, The Co was already out the door, speed-walking down the hall.

It had only been a few hours since this afternoon's pool bar\tequila\wheelchair incident. It seemed that the absinthe was aiding his swift recovery.

"Where are we going?" I asked, as we walked out of the hotel, receiving several dirty looks from the staff along the way.

"The Nutty Brown," he said. "There's a Mark McKeith concert there; should be good."

"A country concert? Okay."

"You have to drive, though," The Co said. "Things don't usually end well when I drive."

"Agreed."

The Co is a drunk. He basically goes from one bender to the next with short interludes of recovery, such as, bathtub naps and hung-over airplane rides. As a result of his lifestyle, he has a history of getting himself into all sorts of ridiculous situations.

Previous incidents include: wedging his car into the corner of a house with a stop sign stuck in the windshield (naturally there was jail time and a license suspension to follow), waking up naked in some guy's bed (according to him this incident was never to be spoken of again), and repeatedly driving up over the curb at the end of the block he lived on, through someone's yard, and running over the same set of bushes every single time he drove home (the homeowners were beyond fed up at this point.)

How he maintains a valid driver's license and manages to not get banned from society in general is beyond me. But it seemed as though, at least The Co may finally be catching on to the fact the he doesn't belong behind the wheel; EVER!

That is especially after his most recent incident that had taken place the previous Saturday, while on an overnight in Gary, Indiana, The Co's hometown. I had spent the evening hanging out with him and some of his friends.

After spending several hours watching The Co down a couple handles of rum, I was tired. It was time to head back to my hotel.

The Co was staying at a buddy's house who lived nearby and was insistent on driving his own car there. I was by far the soberer of the two of us, so I decided to follow The Co to his destination in my rental, and then head to my hotel. We were going less than two miles; all I had to do was make sure he was parked in the driveway, the keys were out of the ignition, and then continue on my way. It seemed simple enough. I failed miserably.

So there we were thirty seconds into the drive, and The Co was already driving on the wrong side of the road. After a half mile of honking and flashing my lights to get his attention, he finally moved over to the right side of the road. I don't think he moved over because I got his attention, nor do I think he realized that he was on the wrong side of the road; I think it was just pure coincidence that he drifted over.

We finally made it to the right street, and he pulled into the driveway right before his buddy's house. I pulled into the correct driveway and looked over at The Co's car in front of the neighbor's house. Now, I wasn't very familiar with this area, so I started to question whether or not I was at the right house.

I sat there for minute looking at The Co's car, waiting for him to get out, but he never did. I walked over figuring he had just reclined the seat and went to sleep right there in the driveway. When I looked in to check on him, I found the car empty. *He's not in the car; he parked in the wrong driveway—maybe there's something I don't know. Does he know these neighbors? Is this the right house and I'm in the wrong driveway?* I thought I was in the right place, but this was The Co's turf; he should have known better than I did.

After knocking on the door and speaking to the homeowner, I learned that he didn't know The Co, nor was The Co in his house. After a brief search of the area, I gave up. I got in my rental and drove back to the hotel.

Nine a.m. the following morning, the phone rang. It's The Co. "WAAAAA! You won't believe what I did!" he screamed into my ear. "I just woke up on some guy's couch!"

He proceeded to tell me the story. I found out that the door that I had knocked on the night before, the driveway The Co had parked in, The Co had been asleep inside that house. The door had been unlocked, and he just walked in, not realizing he was at the wrong house. He had slept the whole night there on the guy's couch till being woken up in the morning with a twelve gauge.

The cops were now involved, which led to a tense scene in the front lawn of this guy's house. The Co, who was wearing ill-fitting leather pants and a pink Led Zeppelin t-shirt (really a sight to be seen), argued with the angry homeowner, who was pacing back and forth in a bathrobe, twelve gauge still in hand, threatening prosecution.

Two very large Gary Indiana Police Officers, who found the whole situation to be quite amusing, ultimately sided with The Co on account that, if you don't lock your front door, waking up to find a leather-clad drunk sleeping on your couch is a reasonable situation to find yourself in.

The Co wasn't about to change his behavior, but at least he was now requesting a chauffeur, when available. So even though I wasn't really in the mood to go out tonight, I drove us, mainly because if The Co ended up in jail, I wouldn't have a co-pilot to fly with in the morning.

The Chief would blame me for this. "You should have kept an eye on him," he'd say. You see it's the captain's responsibility to babysit their co-pilot while on overnights.

We pulled up in front of the Nutty Brown on the outskirts of Austin. The place was packed, and the crowd was very country. As we looked around, it was hard to spot anyone who wasn't wearing cowboy boots. The Co and I were from the Midwest, so we don't own cowboy boots. While waiting in line to get in, someone actually asked me, "Where's your boots, son?" I was wearing the same flip-flops I wore to work, and The Co was wearing tennis shoes. Neither were considered to be acceptable types of footwear around there.

"I don't have any boots," I answered.

"You don't have any boots?" the cowboy questioned, and with genuine concern he asked, "What are ya, a Yankee?"

"I don't know?"

"Well, where ya'll from?"

"Ohio."

"Oh yeah, you're a Yankee. Everyone north of Waco's all Yankees."

I felt a little out of place here and sensed trouble from the start. Not to mention The Co's rapidly deteriorating condition as he continued to drink absinthe from a flask.

"What's the deal with this guy?" the cowboy asked, pointing at The Co.

"He's a Yankee, too," I answered.

"Huh," the cowboy shrugged his shoulders, not knowing what to make of us.

Once we got inside, we ran into more trouble. Apparently, some obscure Texas law states that in certain counties you must have a Texas ID to buy alcohol. Personally, I think this "law" was made up on the spot, just for The Co and me. Regardless of that, this was a problem since neither of us had Texas IDs. After a losing argument with the bartender and the manager, we found a solution to the problem. We had to pay a middleman with a Texas license a commission to buy our beer for us.

After we had that problem was behind us, the real trouble of the night would involve an autographed picture of Mark McKeith, the singer we came to see. The Co had bought a CD from him prior to the show, which included a free autographed picture. The Co had stuck the picture in his shirt pocket without even looking at it, and shortly thereafter he lost the CD.

Later that night, during the show, while The Co was dancing— or swaying, depending on how you look at it—he stumbled into a lumberjack who was standing in front of us. I knew he was a lumberjack because he was wearing a Stihl hat and a red flannel shirt. He was furious, and looked like he was ready to either chop down a tree or beat The Co's ass, whichever came first.

The angry lumberjack turned around and shoved The Co, which knocked the autographed photo out of his pocket. As The Co lay on the ground, the lumberjack reached down and picked up the photo. He stared at it in disbelief. "Why do you have this?" he asked angrily.

"It came with the CD I bought," The Co responded, as he struggled to stand up.

It was at that moment I caught a glimpse of the photo. It was an autographed picture of Mark McKeith in grape-smugglers lying suggestively on the hood of a Trans-am.

"We're leaving," I said, grabbing The Co who was near blackout drunk at this point.

As we walked away leaving the lumberjack and photo behind, The Co whined, "Why are we leaving?"

"'Cause you were about to be the victim of a gay bashing," I informed him.

The Co wanted to go to another bar, but I'd had enough for one day. "Let's just get some food then go back to the hotel." I suggested.

"Fine." The Co grumbled.

So, we made a quick stop at a twenty-four-hour pancake house, but The Co got us kicked out before we even sat down. He passed out, and face planted into the front door as we were walking in. When he hit the ground, I looked up to see the restaurant manager staring at us from behind the counter, with a look that said, "Don't you dare come in here."

"Good job," I said to The Co, "you just ruined our hopes for getting any food. I picked him up off the ground, dragged him across the parking lot, and loaded him into the backseat of our rental.

Upon arriving back at the hotel, The Co was conscious again and completely belligerent. While passing through the lobby, he started screaming gibberish at the woman at the front desk, who stood in shock with the phone in her hand, probably wondering if she should dial 911. Then he hit the emergency stop button on the escalator while some people were riding down, sending them tumbling. "What's your problem, man?" One of them yelled at The Co, who just stood there, wobbling, completely unaware of what he had just done.

"I'm sorry," I jumped in, not wanting the situation to get any worse than it already was. I grabbed The Co by the back of his shirt and led him towards the elevator.

Once I managed to get him into his room, he immediately went straight to his bag, pulled out a fresh bottle of Absinthe, and slumped on the bed.

"More?"

He unscrewed the cap and took a long slug from the bottle.

"Try to get some sleep," I told him, and set the alarm clock on his nightstand.

I left The Co and returned to my own room. It had been a long night, and it was time for bed. After all, we had to work in the morning.

- 3 -
It's a Rodeo Up Here

As worthless as The Co was, flying with Chip was worse. The guy was a punching bag for life, and I was stuck with him all night.

The Co had called in sick again tonight, claiming he had been struck by lightning while washing his car. That may seem hard to believe. You might ask why he was washing his car during a thunderstorm. Bottom line is that he was running out of excuses.

The previous week, he claimed to have been hit by a logging truck while riding his bike. He said he became entangled with the truck somehow and was dragged "for no less than forty miles." This obviously resulted in a no-call, no-show, but, of course, he got out of it with just a warning because he claimed he had dropped his phone after about the first mile, leaving him unable to call.

Previous excuses he has used for his poor attendance included: "I was in a coma," "I got the plague and I've been in quarantine," and "I had to make several trips to Coinstar because my ashtray was overflowing with spare change." I really don't understand why The Chief was buying this crap.

While flying with The Co definitely had its downsides, tonight I needed him. Flying with Chip was going to be miserable: bottom line was, the guy was just afraid of flying. Even more than that, he was afraid of thunderstorms, and that's what we'd be dealing with all night. Chip would piss himself, I was sure of it.

A few years prior, Chip had been in a single-engine Cessna that had caught on fire when he was a flight instructor, and he had never mentally recovered from it. He and his student were on approach to land at some small airport in Michigan when the plane burst into flames. He landed the plane, then he and his student tucked and rolled out of the side doors onto the runway while the plane was still moving. They both stood up just in time to watch their burning airplane ghost ride off the end of the runway.

The plane rolled down into a ditch where it continued to burn until it was no longer recognizable as an airplane.

Chip and his student walked away from that incident suffering only minor cuts and scratches, but, emotionally, he was scarred for life. I guess he figured he should have died that day. I can't blame him for being afraid, but I'll never quite understand why Chip continued to fly when he was so damn scared of it.

Since that incident Chip has made a reputation for himself in the aviation industry as a guy who buckles under pressure, often losing control of the airplane during simulated emergencies in training. Prior to Checkflight hiring him, he had interviewed at several other airlines, all of which turned him down.

Airlines assess prospective pilot candidates by subjecting them to a simulator evaluation, in which they are asked to demonstrate the ability to handle various emergency situations. Chip often lacks in this department, anything out of the ordinary causes him to either freeze up at the controls or make sudden erratic maneuvers, which would usually result in him crashing the simulator.

While every other airline that Chip had interviewed at, found his inabilities to fly under pressure to be the nail in the coffin in his interview. The Chief, however, found Chip's willingness to work for minimum wage to be of great value to the company; so much so, that he was willing to completely overlook Chip's simulator evaluation, in which he had graveyard spiraled the plane into the ground during a simulated alternator failure.

And as if that wasn't enough, Chip then topped off his performance by pissing himself, quite possibly making him the first person in history to be offered a job while wearing urine-soaked khakis.

And *that* is who I'd be flying with tonight.

In Chip's defense his simulator evaluation had been a shining success in comparison to The Co's, which ended promptly when he lost control of the plane during the first takeoff, ran off the runway, and crashed.

The Chief also found this performance to be "easily overlookable" in comparison to the fact that The Co appeared to be a person of low moral standards, and was also willing to work for minimum wage.

When I walked out to the airplane, I found Chip in his seat, already strapped in by all five points of the harness, including the nut-strap cinched tight. First of all, this went against my very firm policy on seat belt and harness use which clearly states: wear the lap belt. For severe turbulence, put on the shoulder harnesses, and the nut strap is only for when you are definitely crashing.

"We're not leaving for another thirty minutes," I told him. "You don't have to be buckled up yet."

"I'm fine," he said. "I'll just wait here."

Great, this was the type of shit I'd be dealing with all night.

But, as much as Chip annoyed me, there was one good thing about him. He was obsessed with pre-flighting, which meant I didn't have to do it. When I flew with Chip, I knew that the pre-flight checks on the airplane would be done well.

Chip's view on pre-flighting was, "the airplane is broken until it's proven otherwise." This guy would show up two hours before the flight and pour over every detail of the plane. I swear he would spend twenty minutes just checking the lights; I don't even know how that's possible. Most people didn't spend twenty minutes on the whole airplane. He would even wipe down and re-grease the landing gear struts before each flight; he brought his own grease and everything. It was ridiculous, but, maybe if Chip had been with me in Dallas, he would have noticed that the tire was falling off the rim. The Co sure as hell didn't.

The Co's pre-flight consisted of walking up to the airplane at the last minute, getting in, and saying, "I didn't see anything wrong with the plane when I walked up." Then again, The Co has also pre-flighted by saying, "Well it was fine when we left it yesterday."

"I've got a few discrepancies with the plane that I found during the pre-flight." Chip said. "I'd like to discuss them with you."

"Well, if you're sitting in the plane ready to go, then I'm sure everything's fine." I said. Knowing that there is no way Chip would get in and buckle up, unless everything was okay.

"Yes, but when I came out to the plane, I found the left engine's oil very low." Chip's voice shuddered when he spoke those words.

The very thought of someone operating the engine with less than the prescribed amount of oil terrified him.

"It leaks." I said. "Did you fill it?"

"Yes." He adjusted his glasses. The cold sweat rushing over him was causing them to slide off his nose.

"Anything else?" I asked.

His hand shook as he pointed at the left engine. "There was a lot of smoke and backfiring when I started it up."

"Yeah, that one just does that." I assured him. "It smoothes out after a few minutes."

While an engine smoking and backfiring might alarm the average person, I'd been a freight dog long enough to be immune to these kinds of things.

"Okay captain, if you think it's good to go," Chip said, "but, I'd like to speak with you about the weather and our routing, too."

I let out a sigh. "Go ahead."

I had wanted to go back inside to check my email, to see if I'd gotten anymore rejection letters from other airlines I'd been applying to, but it looked like this was going to take a few minutes. "Brief" is not he word I would use to describe Chip's weather briefing's, this was another glaring difference between Chip and The Co.

The Co's weather briefings were just as half-assed as his pre-flight. His attitude towards getting a weather briefing being; "no matter what the weather is we're going anyway, so why even bother checking it." He would glance at the radar from a distance as he walked by and say, "Weather looks good."

Chip's weather briefing, on the other hand, was beyond ridiculous. He spent hours on the computer pouring over every bit of data. He kept notebooks filled with wind data that he would use to plan the route and altitude that would give us the lowest fuel burn possible. And, due to the thunderstorms that were out there tonight, he had meticulously plotted two possible routes that would keep us well clear of the weather.

Chip's fuel burn obsession carried over into his daily commute to work as well. He knew every traffic light on his route to the airport, and he knew the average traffic volumes for every road at any given time. He would calculate the exact minute he needed to leave his house to get to the airport burning the least possible amount of gas.

I listened to him drone on for several minutes about this crap, and he even tried to engage me in his madness. "What altitude do you think we should fly at?" Chip asked, though he obviously already had the correct one in mind.

"Which ever one is on the flight plan." I said. I could care less about fuel burn.

I didn't care about saving money for Checkflight anymore. This frustrated Chip, but he pressed on. "Well, do you think we should take the north route or the south route around the weather?" He asked.

"We'll be flying direct." I told him.

"But— that'll take us through the weather."

"Oh, there's the courier." I interrupted, seeing my chance to escape. "I'm gonna go help him load."

Once airborne, Chip continued with his weather spiel.

"Let's talk about something else." I said. "What else is new?"

"Well— My wife left me," he whined.

I didn't know if this would be an improvement over the weather conversation, but at least it was a change of pace. Chip's personal life had been a roller coaster of bad news lately, this could be interesting. "Again?" I asked. "What happened this time?"

"Well, she ran off to Florida with some guy she met on HALO."

"You mean like on Xbox?"

"Yeah, I guess he was pretty good. I suck at that game," Chip said. "If I had been better, I bet she would have stayed with me."

I didn't even know how to respond to this. What kind of screwed up world does Chip live in where a lack of video game skill is ending his relationships?

"Well, keep practicing," I said, "that way you'll be good enough for the next girl."

This was typical of Chip's life lately. Ever since his first wife left him, his life had become increasingly unpredictable. Chip has always been this shy, dweeby guy. He was still that way, but now he was nuts too.

Chip's quiet life got turned upside down a few months ago when his first wife, whom he had a son with, confessed to him after ten years of marriage that she had been cheating on him the whole time. The real shocker came when she told him that she had been cheating on him with his dad, and that his son was actually his brother. I'll give you a minute to digest that.

THE GUY HAD BEEN RAISING HIS BROTHER AS HIS SON FOR EIGHT YEARS!

Chip went a little crazy after that, which has led to a string of very odd behavior. He had hooked up with our new janitor in the back of her car in the parking lot, who, I might add, was no prize. She looked like she had been ridden hard and put up wet, to use a phrase I had learned down in Texas. The good part was she drove a convertible, so we all got to witness the horror show.

It was her first day working here, so she got fired. Unfortunately, Chip still works here. He got off the hook with just a verbal warning to watch his behavior on company property.

Chip and that janitor got married later that day. That was two weeks ago; guess it didn't last.

"How long ago did she leave you?" I asked.

"About a week ago," Chip said. "We had planned our whole lives together."

"So, you were married for a whole week and it didn't work out, that's a shame."

Things got quiet in the plane for a few minutes while Chip sobbed.

"So, what happened?" I asked.

"Well," he said, "I guess I had it coming."

"Do tell. Were you two having problems, I mean other than the video game issues?"

"Well, there was a problem with one of her dogs; I kicked him out. I came home one day to find another puppy in the apartment; she was always rescuing puppies."

"How many dogs did she have?"

"Fifteen including this new one and she brought them all to my place when she moved in with me. I'm not crazy about dogs in the first place, and this new dog she named Phillip was a terrorist, I was sure of it. Within a few days our apartment was reduced to rubble by this five-pound Dachshund, rendering it unlivable. Between the destruction of property, wanton defecation, and the noise violations from his constant barking, we were on the verge of being evicted. I had to do something. I mean, it got to the point where we were forced to wear shoes in the house, to avoid stepping in the land mines that turned the carpet into a major health issue. So, one day while Phillip

Hauling Checks

looked me straight in the eye as he laid cable on the living room rug, I decided he had overstayed his welcome. I figured she would never even notice he was gone. I mean she had so many dogs. The time had come to pin a twenty to his collar and wish him luck. So that's what I did. He walked away and we never saw him again. But, when she found out what I had done, she lost it. She said she thought she knew me, and kept screaming, 'How could you do this?' She said she could never forgive me, but the next day, she was fine like it never happened. I figured it had blown over, until she left me."

"And all of this happened within a week?"

"Best week of my life, and I threw it all away."

"Well, keep your head up. Things will get better for you."

While Chip's problems were very entertaining, I'd had enough of listening to his whiney voice, so I turned on the radar. The weather would be approaching soon, and things were about to get interesting. We were flying from St. Louis to Omaha, and there was a huge line of storms in our way, stretching north to south several hundred miles. Not my idea of a good time, but Chip was about to lose his lunch over there, literally, when we started seeing lightning in the distance, Chip began dry heaving. "Dude, are you about to produce some groceries over there?" I asked him.

"I'm fine," he said, "just the hiccups."

Right, I thought.

Just then air traffic control cut in. "Checkflight 101, I'm showing several areas of extreme precip for the next twenty miles along your route of flight. Confirm you have weather radar on board."

I paused before answering, looking down at our weather radar, that was still going through its fifteen-minute warm-up sequence.

While modern weather radars display weather in four colors;

green/light precipitation, yellow/moderate, red/heavy, and magenta/extreme; ours had an old green monochrome display, like an Apple IIe computer. It displayed three shades of green, depicting light, moderate, and heavy precipitation, and flashing dark green for extreme precipitation. The problem was, the screen was so old that all three shades of green looked the same, and the whole thing flickered constantly, making it difficult to distinguish glitches from actual weather. Even worse, the radar dish in the nose of the plane was loose. During turbulence, it would bounce around up there, causing the radar image to shift constantly. One minute, the radar would display a storm cell at our one o'clock position, then with the next sweep of the radar the cell would move to our eleven o'clock position, without any change in the direction of the plane, making it impossible to determine exactly where the cell was, but at least it gave us a ballpark.

The warm-up sequence finished, and the radar screen began filling with different shades and flashes of green. "Yes, we have weather radar on board." I responded.

"Alright Checkflight 101," the controller said, "I haven't had anyone go through the weather yet, everyone else has diverted around it. Let me know if you'd like to divert."

I wasn't about to divert; it would add way too much time to the flight, and we had deadlines to make. "We're good." I said. "We'd like to continue direct to Omaha."

"Okay, Checkflight 101, that's at your discretion."

Chip clearly wanted to divert. "Come on, let's go around it." He begged, but no matter how much he insisted, I wasn't budging.

"What about your fuel burn obsession? If we divert that'll cost us fuel, I'd figure you'd rather go straight through and save gas?"

"Not if it's thunderstorms; I hate storms."

"I can tell, you're turning green."

Chip didn't respond.

Just then, lightning flashed just off our nose. I glanced down at the radar; the screen flickered a few times then went blank, rendering it useless. I tightened my lap belt and turned up the cockpit lights to drown out the lightning. "Here we go!" I yelled, as we entered the weather. The turbulence started to kick up, and heavy rain began to hammer the airplane.

Within seconds, the rain penetrated the cockpit, ready to add its contribution to the ever-increasing mold growth that plagued the thirty-year-old upholstery. It leaked in from every windshield seam, dripping on the instrument panel where puddles quickly formed. My left shoulder was already soaked; I glanced over to see water spraying in through the dry rotted weather stripping that surrounded the side door. I picked my feet up off the floor, resting them higher on the rudder pedals, knowing that before this storm was over the leaking air ducts under our seats would leave the carpet a swampy water-logged mess.

The plane got tossed around like a rag doll as the updrafts and downdrafts took us. I watched our airspeed fluctuate wildly up and down, continually making power adjustments to keep everything within tolerances.

This beaten and battered plane has been through countless thunderstorms in its life as a freighter; the nose and wings showing the scars of hail damage. If it looked that bad on the surface, who knew how mangled things were internally. *Could this be the storm that finally breaks it apart?*

The turbulence worsened. One minute we were nose down, with the power at idle, the airspeed screaming through red line in an updraft; the next we were full power, losing altitude and speed, as a downdraft pushed us towards the ground.

"Damn, it's a rodeo up here! Ask for a block altitude," I told Chip. This would allow us to ride the waves through the storm easier without having to maintain a constant altitude.

Chip didn't say a word.

"Chip, you hear me?" I yelled. I looked over and realized he was catatonic. He sat there in his seat, staring straight ahead like he was looking into the face of a ghost.

"Oh, don't worry I'll do it myself." It seems like no matter who I fly with I always get stuck doing all the work. Damn worthless copilots!

I keyed my mic button. "Center, Checkflight 101; requesting a block."

"Checkflight 101, maintain block five-to-seven thousand." The controller responded.

"Five-to-seven, thanks." I said, letting the plane drift off altitude, wherever the storm chose to take it.

"How's the ride?" The controller asked like a smart ass.

Turbulence hit us so hard my eyeballs shook in their sockets. "Smooth." I responded, sarcastically.

The controller said something back, but I couldn't hear it. There was a roar of blaring static interference over the radios. Lightning flashed as bright as daylight all around us, and Saint Elmo's fire crept up the windscreen. I glanced over my shoulder to see the lights in the rear cargo area flickering on and off as the boxes bounced around back there hitting the light switch.

And that's when I smelled the shit, literally. Chip had shit himself.

The weather was over before long as we punched out the backside of the line but the shit smell would stay for the rest of the night. What was worse was that, when Chip came out of his catatonic state and began speaking to air traffic control again, he started crying on the radio, saying things like "Tell my parents I love them," and "I'm too young to die."

"Will you calm down?" I said. "You're spilling your placenta all over the radio."

I had to pull his headset cords out of the mic jacks to save us from further embarrassment.

After the weather and the turbulence calmed down, Chip started to regain his composure a bit. He didn't make any mention of the unmistakable shit smell. I guess he was hoping that I hadn't noticed.

I stared out the window, daydreaming for a while, watching the lightning fade into the distance behind us. We still had a ways to go till our arrival in Omaha, and I was starting to get bored.

"Do you have any books?" I asked Chip. "I mean, besides that one." He was studying charts in an aviation weather services textbook.

"Oh— you can read some of my notebooks on weather and fuel planning." He said excitedly, while pulling a few of them out of his bag.

"Never mind"

I searched the back-seat pockets and found a "Butt Man" magazine that someone had left behind. I began reading it to pass the time, yet my eyes grew heavier by the minute.

One thing that got tough on those long flights in the middle of the night was staying awake. My head started to bob back and forth as I struggled to keep my eyes open. Every few seconds, I would jerk my head up wondering how long I had been asleep. However, before long, I was asleep, and, in a little while, I would find out that Chip had fallen asleep too…

My eyes opened in a panic as I woke up to the sound of the engines sputtering. Suddenly, the sound was replaced by a high-pitched wail that erupted from Chip. Quickly scanning the instrument panel, I saw red warning lights lit up all over. The right engine had quit, and the left engine was in the process of sputtering out.

"Fuel!" I yelled, springing to action.

We had been asleep so long the outboard fuel tanks had run dry. The right outboard tank was empty, and the left engine was slurping the last drops out of the left outboard tank. There was still fuel in the inboard tanks, but, since we had been asleep rather than monitoring the fuel, we had missed the warning lights that would have told us that the tanks we were running on were almost empty.

I quickly switched the fuel selectors to the inboard tanks and turned the emergency fuel pumps on to get fuel to the dying engines as quickly as possible.

The plane yawed from side to side as the engines roared back to life. Slowly, the red warning lights began to extinguish. Within a minute or so, everything was back to normal, and the plane began to regain the speed it lost during the loss of power.

Just then air traffic control chimed in. "Checkflight 101, is everything alright?" the controller asked.

"Quiet!" I yelled at Chip, who was still screaming like a little girl. I had to backhand his mouth to get him to stop.

"Yup, everything is fine," I said to the controller, trying to sound normal, as if nothing had happened.

"Oh, Okay," the controller said. "It just seemed like you slowed down quite a bit pretty rapidly; looks like you're speeding up again."

"No," I said, trying to play dumb, "we've been at a constant speed; must have been a computer error."

I looked over at Chip who was sitting with both hands clenching his armrests. His pants were wet, and liquid was dripping from the bottom of his seat.

"Why are your pants wet?" I asked.

"I just peed a little," Chip said while still sitting there, frozen face staring straight ahead.

"Everything's fine," I assured him. "We just ran the outboards dry."

Shortly after our little fuel incident, it was time to begin our descent into Omaha. I eased the power back as Omaha approach control vectored us towards the airport. Normally, I would rip the power to idle and dive the plane towards the airport, making near knife-edge turns to line up with the runway. But today, since Chip was on board, I was being gentler than usual. I really didn't want to find out what other types of bodily fluids he could produce.

After a few minutes, we were on the ground.

As soon as I shut down the plane, Chip asked me what our total fuel burn for the flight was. When I told him, he seemed happy. For some reason, that seemed to be the only thing about flying that made Chip happy—getting a good fuel burn. I think it's the only reason he was still flying: he put himself through the torture and fear of being in the air just for the satisfaction of getting a good fuel number at the end.

And I couldn't believe that, as he sat there with his pants soiled, fuel burn was still his primary concern.

I got out to unload the cargo. Chip took his suitcase inside the building to find a restroom so he could get himself cleaned up and put some fresh clothes on that he would most likely soil on the next flight. The guy traveled with a ridiculous amount of luggage. I guess he was prepared to have a clean change of clothes for each flight, if need be.

The courier backed his mini-van up to the airplane as I began to throw the bags and boxes of work out onto the ramp. When he got out of his van, I couldn't believe my eyes. He was one of the strangest characters I'd ever seen in my life.

He was probably in his sixties, and had a grey mullet that stretched halfway down his back. It looked like the haircut a professional wrestler from the eighties would have. His teeth were awful. They stuck out in all different directions. It looked like he had been chewing on bricks. He wore a grey pinstripe suit; only the pinstripes were multi-color pastels with a tie to match. The coat was a knee-length cut, and his shoes appeared to be mustard yellow leather with gold buckles.

I'd met quite a few strange characters at odd hours of the night on dark airport ramps, but this guy topped the list.

"Hello," he said, "and please to meet you, my name is Vladimir."

"Vladimir?" I said. "That's an interesting name. Where are you from?"

I had half expected him to say his name was Jake the Snake or something like that, but I guess Vladimir was fitting.

"My name is Russian," he said, "but I am Hungarian."

"What brought you Nebraska?"

"I always dreamed to live in the plains of United States."

To each his own I thought. "Can I get a picture of you? I always take pictures of the people I meet around the country when I'm traveling."

Actually, I never take pictures of random people I meet, but I had to get a picture of this guy. No one would ever believe me.

"Okay," he said, as he stiffly posed.

I snapped a picture of him with the camera on my phone. "Thanks!" I said.

We finished loading the work in his mini-van, and he left. Chip came out in fresh clothes just in time to miss out on meeting Vladimir.

"You wouldn't believe this courier," I said to Chip, "his mullet was unreal, and he was wearing a suit with blue, pink, and yellow pinstripes!"

I showed Chip the picture I had taken with my phone, but he didn't seem amused. He was already starting to worry about the next flight. We were heading back east and we would have to cross that same line of thunderstorms again on our way home.

- 4 -
Standby

There is nothing more exciting in the life of a cargo pilot than a night of standby. It involves spending ten consecutive hours sitting at the airport doing nothing. Airlines need to have pilots on standby at all times in case another pilot calls in sick. At Checkflight, since The Co worked here, this was extremely important. Actually, The Co called in sick so often that he needed his own personal standby pilot; this being Chip's primary role at this company.

Checkflight, also needed pilots on standby in case a customer needed an extra flight at the last minute, due to extra bulk or special shipments. Standby pilots can also be used to reposition airplanes in the case that one of our planes broke down somewhere. Of course, this happened constantly. Checkflight operated more empty maintenance repositioning flights, than cargo carrying revenue flights. Maybe if our planes were better maintained we wouldn't waste so much money flying around empty.

Save pennies and waste thousands, that's how The Chief operated.

I arrived at the airport at nine p.m. for my night of mandatory standby. If nothing popped up for me to do through the night, I'd spend most of the night sleeping in a recliner in the pilots' lounge and I could go home at seven a.m. Sometimes that happened, sometimes it didn't.

There had been times where I'd sat there all night only to be sent out on a flight at six-thirty in the morning, just before it was time to go home. That was the worst. There had been other times where dispatch kept me up all night, telling me they might have a flight for me to do in thirty minutes, but it never happened. This got annoying because they could never seem to make up their minds on what they wanted to do.

The most important thing about standby days was to bring something to do. You had to bring a book, music, *some*thing. Otherwise, you could get very bored real quick. We had a tube TV in the pilots' lounge, but the only thing on at four in the morning was "Girls Gone Wild" infomercials, and that horrible steel drum reggae music was starting to get to me.

The tube TV was also equipped with a VCR, but I had no idea how to track down VHS tapes in this day-in-age. The only tape we had was The Co's copy of "Cheech and Chong's: Up in Smoke" which we have now watched at least six-hundred times.

I walked into the dispatch office to check in and was greeted by our dispatcher Karen. "Hey Karen, I'm checking in for standby," I said.

The dispatch office was dark and filled with several cubicles. Karen was the only one in the room, the rest of the cubicles sat empty, reminisce of a busier time

Karen was full of shit, and I knew I was going to be stuck here for a while listening to her far-fetched stories about her new husband.

"Hey," Karen said, as she typed on her computer, "I got you checked in."

"Thanks," I said as I tried to walk out of the room before she could launch into another one of her tall tales.

"Did I tell you about Sherman?" she asked catching me before I could get out the door.

She claimed that her new husband's name was Sherman, which quite frankly sounded like the only thing that may be legit about the whole thing. You would think if she was going to make up a husband, she would have made up a more common name for him. But, then again, I think maybe she had thought about that and made up an uncommon name on purpose.

"No," I said feigning interest, "what's he been up to?"

"Well," she said excitedly, "he's running for Congress!"

"Congress? That's unbelievable!" *Literally.*

"Yea, I'm so excited. We're going to be moving to Washington, and he's going to be rich. Guess I won't have to work here anymore! I'm gonna be hanging out at the White House with the First Lady. Maybe we could even go shopping together!"

This was exactly the type of crap she was always coming up with. Now he was running for Congress? It wasn't like I had anything better to do at the moment, except sit here and listen to her. But I still couldn't help feeling that this was a serious waste of time.

Every other day, Sherman was supposedly right on the verge of getting some great new job, and Karen was always just about to quit her job because Sherman was about to make her rich. Only it was a different, great new job every time, usually in a completely different industry. And, more importantly, none of it ever materialized, and Karen was still here.

Sometimes it was some sort of get-rich-quick scheme. A few

months ago, Karen had told me that Sherman fell in a supermarket parking lot, breaking his leg in three different places. She claimed he had two heart attacks as a result of the fall, was breathing on a vent, and paralyzed on his left side. She claimed that they were going to sue the supermarket for two million and then she'd be quitting here because she'd be rich.

Two days later she told me that he had made a full recovery and was released from the hospital and walking around. How do you recover from being paralyzed in two days? The story got even better when she told me that, during the time he was in the hospital, he played a flight simulator game on the computer and earned his pilot's license.

"That's great" I told her egging her on, "I got my pilot's license in two days by playing a computer game too!"

When I asked her if they got the two million from the supermarket yet, she told me, "No, we told them we don't need it anymore 'cause now that Sherman has his pilot's license, he's getting a job flying for a major passenger airline based in Antarctica. So, he's going to be making so much money they can keep the two million."

"Antarctica?" I said, "I didn't know they had passenger flights there. Why doesn't he get a job here at Checkflight?"

Karen then informed me that there are lots of flights in Antarctica and that their airport is very busy.

"Plus," she said, "they are going to pay him two hundred thousand down there, and they won't pay that much here."

I felt tempted to commend her on her ability to keep a straight face while telling me this, but decided against it. "Good point," I told her, "tell him I said good luck. Do you think he can get me a job down there?"

"No," she said, "they only want him, because he's so good. They said he's one of the best pilots they've ever seen."

"I understand," I said. "Good for him!"

A few days later, when I asked her for a follow up to this story, she told me that Sherman was no longer taking the job flying in Antarctica. When I asked her why not, she told me it was because aviation was a dying industry.

"People just don't need to fly anymore," she said.

Yeah, I thought. *Teleporting is really taking off these days.*

Sherman was also supposedly in the army and was always on the verge of deployment. For as long as Karen had been talking about Sherman, he had always been just a few days away from being deployed to Iraq. It never actually happened though, and she always had a different excuse for why not.

I think she just liked the attention.

"So, what about this running for Congress?" I asked. "What part of Congress is he running for?"

"The House of Representatives," she said. "They want him there really bad."

"Wow! So, is he preparing for his campaign? What party is he running for?"

"Well, he's a Democrat, but he doesn't need to run."

"Why's that?"

"Well, they just really want him, and nobody wants to be in Congress right now, so no one is going to run against him. They just told him he can have it."

"Wow, I didn't know you could do that! I always thought it was pretty tough to get into Congress!"

"Yeah, usually, but not for him. He knows a lot of people."

"Cool. I wish I had those kinds of connections."

Just then the phone rang, and Karen had to answer it; this was my chance to escape. "I'll be in the lounge if you need me," I said as I walked out.

I went down to the pilots' lounge and brushed the crumbs off of one of the recliners so I could sit down. Ever since the janitor that Chip hooked up with was fired, we haven't had one. The Chief had decided, after that, "Employing a janitor is an unnecessary expense." Now, the whole building was disgusting. The pilots lounge was completely garbage strewn, it looked like a place where a bunch of hoarders hung out. There were about ten pizza boxes piled on top of the tiny trash can in the corner, I seriously doubt that anyone was ever going to empty it again. People have just continued to pile trash on top of it, some are now just throwing their trash on the floor. A small mountain of McDonald's bags was forming in one corner, half of a lasagna sat in a Tupperware container on the table, and there were even coffee stains on the walls. Every time I came in here, there seemed to be some sort of debris on every single recliner, it's like people just came in here specifically to eat crackers.

I pulled my hood over my head so I could lean back without my hair touching the upholstery. A little while later, The Co, who was scheduled to be on standby as well, showed up late as usual. He immediately jumped into one of the recliners, right on top of a spilled pile of rice, and went to sleep. I tried to fall asleep as well, but I couldn't. I had flown all last night and slept all day today, so I wasn't tired, but I sure was bored.

I spent most of the night sitting there in the pilots' lounge, listening to music on my iPod and doing crossword puzzles. I kept counting the hours off till my standby time would be over, and I could go home. But, at about five in the morning, tragedy struck. Karen was calling The Co and me over the PA, and I knew what that meant. I was only two hours away from going home and now I was going to have to fly somewhere, and I probably wouldn't be back here by seven.

The blaring PA system had failed to wake The Co from his nap, so I left him behind, and went to the dispatch office to see what Karen wanted.

She told me that another crew's plane had broken down, so The Co and I would have to cover for them. The run she wanted us to fly would have us working well into the morning, way past our duty time limits. Pilots, by law, are only allowed to be on duty for fourteen hours. But that didn't matter at Checkflight. The Chief even had a sign on the wall in his office that read "DUTY TIME LIMITS ARE FOR CRYBABIES!" But I was going down to his office to protest anyway.

Before I walked out of dispatch, Karen said, "Guess what?"

"What?" I said. I was fire pissed, and in no mood for this.

"Sherman is getting a job with the Montana Border Patrol! Isn't that exciting?"

"Very exciting! But how is he going to be on the Montana Border Patrol when he has to be in Washington for Congress?"

I walked out before she could give me an answer. I marched straight down to The Chief's office to protest. I knew it would get me nowhere, but I was tired of being forced into these things. I was already tired, and now I had another ten hours ahead of me.

"This is bullshit!" I said as I walked into The Chief's office.

"What is?" The Chief asked. He barely even looked up to acknowledge my presence, as he continued crunching numbers on a calculator. The folding table that he used as a desk was a cluttered mess, most likely of unpaid bills.

"Making me do this flight," I said. "It's going to take me way past fourteen hours of duty."

"Did you read the sign?" The Chief asked as he pointed blindly to the poster on the wall.

The Chief's walls were filled with all sorts of inspirational messages. Another sign read, "YOU MUST BE THIS TALL TO TAKE VACATION." It had a line, a height mark eight feet up, near the ceiling.

"Yes, I've seen the sign," I said, "but—."

He looked up at me; his eyes were bloodshot and the harsh fluorescent lighting glared off his bald head. "So, you're aware of the policy and you decided to come down here and complain anyway?"

"Well I—."

"Thanks for doing the flight for us," he said cutting me off again. "That'll be all." He motioned as if shooing me out the door. I left without saying anything else. I knew this would be pointless. I don't know why I bothered.

I went down to the pilots' lounge and woke up The Co. He wasn't very happy about being woken up. I practically had to drag him to the airplane.

Because we were covering flights for another crew whose plane had broken down at the last minute, we were already behind schedule. We now had to hurry to try to make up as much time as possible.

After making the first pickup in Philly, the next stop was Baltimore. We had to drop off work as well as pick up more that we would be taking down to Richmond. But there was another delay.

The courier who was bringing the work to us in Baltimore wasn't there. We were late so he really should have been here by now.

Any time a courier is late, we have to report it to dispatch immediately. "Alright," Karen said, "keep waiting, and I'll give him a call and see if I can find out where he is. I'll give you a call back if I locate him."

"We'll be here." I said.

I sat down on the curb in the parking lot to wait. About twenty minutes later, a murdered-out Honda CRX came tearing into the parking lot. The ridiculous glass pack exhaust screamed ninety horsepower. *Must be the missing courier.*

"You the…uhh…Checkflight pilot?" The driver asked when he got out. He looked pale, and his speech was slurred.

"Yup."

"Sorry I'm…uhh, late," he said, as he quickly grabbed three bank bags out of his trunk. "Here's the work."

I took the bags from him. "What happened?" I asked, "Where have you been?"

"Uhh…I had a little problem on the way here. I…uhh…couldn't make it to the airport in one shot."

He's probably on drugs, I thought. Then asked, "Why not?"

He stared down at his shoes, not wanting to make eye contact, then said, "Well…uhh…I kinda got the runs."

"Oh, well, that sucks."

"Yeah, I've been blowing mud all night. I had to make three rest stops on the way here." He paused for a moment then looked up at me and said, "All you can eat oysters; it seemed like a good idea at the time."

I said, "Yeah, that always seems like a good idea at the time. I mean, why wouldn't you eat all you can eat oysters?"

"I've been shitting blood, and I'm starting to get worried," he unnecessarily informed me, obviously opening up a bit.

"That's not good. You should probably go to the hospital."

"Probably. Is there a bathroom in this place?"

"Yeah, there's one inside." I pointed towards the door.

The courier made a b-line for the door. "Thanks," he said.

I called dispatch to let Karen know that the missing courier had shown up.

Anytime a flight has a late departure, the reason for it has to be recorded, which is put in a report for the customer. If we are late, the banks want to know exactly why. "I want the report to state: 'Late departure due to the runs,'" I told Karen.

"Okay," she said, "I'll put that in the report."

"And, we may want to start looking for a new courier in Baltimore, cause this one might die. He's pooping blood."

"Okay," she said, "I'll make a note of it. Have a good flight."

Now airborne again, we were even further behind schedule, and, the more behind we got, the longer it would be until I got to go to sleep. I was getting more aggravated by the minute because of this.

I jammed the engine controls forward, running the airplane at weekend power*, so we could squeeze every bit of speed out of it we could get.

*- Weekend power means full throttle even if that takes the engines over redline. This may result in airspeed exceeding the maximum speed for the airplane, which would set off a warning horn. If that happens, you just pull the circuit breaker for the warning horn, disabling it. This would allow you to over-speed the airplane without the annoyance of that pesky horn.

Weekend power got its name because no one wants to fly on the weekend, so, if you have to, you fly full power, getting the flight over with as fast a possible so you can go home. Some pilots have also used the terms "Horn Fridays," and "Over-speed Sundays."

Our troubles and delays were far from being over. The biggest delay of the day was yet to come. The problem that would really ruin our day would happen on our second-to-last flight, on our way from Richmond to Charlotte.

It was now into the morning hours, and the sun was rising high into the sky. It was past my bed time, and we were well beyond our fourteen-hour duty time limit. We still had a few hours of flying left, yet I was starting to feel some relief that the end was finally in sight. Little did I know how much worse things were about to get.

I glanced out the side window as I struggled to stay awake. Suddenly, something caught my attention that instantly woke me up. There was oil running out of the left engine. Not just a small leak like there always was. This was a steady flow that trailed down the top of the engine cowling and off the back of the wing.

I watched the oil flow for a moment, wondering if I was dreaming. I rubbed my eyes and slapped my face. *Nope, it's definitely happening.*

"Wake up!" I said to The Co. "We've got a problem."

"That's fine," The Co mumbled in his sleep, "you can take care of it."

I quickly scanned the gauges for the left engine and found that the oil pressure was dropping, and the oil temperature was rising. This confirmed that we were losing a large quantity of oil quickly. There was no way of knowing how much we had lost already, but, judging from the extremely low oil pressure, it wouldn't be long before the engine quit.

The proper procedure in this circumstance is to shut down the left engine. If it lost all of its oil, the engine would seize up, destroying itself. By shutting it down prior to that happening, the engine could be saved, the oil leak could be repaired, and the engine reused.

I'd had enough for one day though. I was pretty disgruntled at this point and decided that I didn't care if the engine was destroyed.

"Let them pay for a new engine," I growled. "That'll teach them."

I left the doomed engine at weekend power; I figured I'd just run the hell out of it till it blew up. This kind of abuse of the engines, which happened on a daily basis, was a big part of the reason the planes had so many problems in the first place. That, combined with the lack of proper maintenance, of course. But when a company constantly treated you as poorly as Checkflight did, it became hard to care about taking care of their airplanes.

After a few minutes, the oil pressure dropped to zero, the temperature was well beyond red line, and suddenly the engine screeched to a halt.

We were now operating single engine, which was an emergency.

I decided; screw Checkflight's policy on not declaring emergencies, and I declared. I wanted to make as big a stink of this as possible. We were only a short distance from our destination of Charlotte at this point, and I was currently in contact with Charlotte approach control.

"Charlotte approach," I said into the mic, "this is Checkflight 101 declaring an emergency. Our left engine quit."

"Roger that Checkflight 101; what sort of assistance will you be requiring?"

"We would like priority handling into Charlotte, and you can roll the trucks."

Rolling the trucks meant that the fire trucks would line the runway as we landed, ready to surround the airplane, and provide fire rescue assistance. I doubted that this would actually be necessary, but I was going for the works on this one. I wanted to make sure this plane was grounded; that way we couldn't finish the route and dispatch would have to get us a hotel. At this point going to sleep was all I cared about.

A few minutes later we landed safely and stopped the plane on the runway; without delay the fire trucks surrounded us.

I shut the plane down and got out to speak with them.

"Is that guy alright?" one of the firemen asked, pointing to The Co who was still asleep in the plane. He had slept through the whole thing.

"Oh him," I said, "yeah, he's fine. That's my copilot; he's just sleeping."

"Did he sleep through the emergency landing?" the fireman asked, obviously a little concerned that a crew member was asleep on the job, and during an emergency landing for that matter.

"He's really tired," I said. "It's been a long night."

I quickly changed the subject and spoke with them for a few more minutes about the engine failure. I was able to convince them that the situation was under control, and finally they left.

Once again, we had to be towed to the ramp by a tug. I chose to ride in the airplane this time, as I had nothing to say to the tug driver.

My usual series of phone calls began with dispatch; I had to let them know what had happened and inform them that we couldn't finish the route. Karen had gone off duty, and Barbara answered the phone.

"I haven't made yet today," Barbara told me. She was always informing everyone on the current status of her bowel movements.

"That's too bad, Barbara," I said, "but we've got a bit of a problem here."

I filled Barbara in on what had happened, she said she would be sending another crew, in another plane, to recover the work and finish the route. But she insisted that we stay there and watch the work until our backup arrived. I wasn't happy about this, because who knew how long it would take them to get here? But I agreed to wait.

"Could you book us a hotel please?" I asked her, "So that once the other plane arrives, we can go to bed?"

"Sure," she said.

"Thanks Barbara, and good luck with the pooping," I told her, before letting her go.

I tried to call The Chief to let him know about the situation, but there was no answer, so I just left him a message. "This is 101; you're plane's broke. Call me back."

After that, I called maintenance and let Tony know that the plane was grounded. As usual, he wasn't happy about this.

"Lost all your oil, huh?" he said. "Boy, these planes are really breaking down today."

"Tony, all of the planes break down every day," I said. "When is the last time a day went by when an airplane didn't lose all its oil?"

"Are you sure it's seized? Try cranking the starter and see if it will turn over."

"It's not going to turn over, Tony. The oil is all over the outside of the airplane."

"Alright, I guess it has to be replaced. Let me see if I can't find someone down there to fix it. I'll give you a call back."

Just minutes later my phone rang. It was Tony. "That was quick," I said.

"Yeah, we got lucky," he said. "They have a spare engine on hand down there. Someone should be there in a few minutes to tow the plane to maintenance."

Since all the work was still on the airplane, The Co and I had to unload it onto the ramp, so they could pull the plane into the maintenance hangar.

Of course, I unloaded while The Co supervised.

Just about the time I finished unloading, a mechanic showed up with a tug to take the airplane. "Is this the plane with the seized engine?" He asked.

"Yup," I said. "It's the left one."

"Man, what's up with your maintenance department?" he asked, sounding a little shaken, "some guy called me and threatened to murder my family if I didn't fix this plane immediately."

"Yeah, that's Tony, sorry about that."

"Look I don't want any trouble. We'll fix your plane, free of charge, as requested."

"Thanks, and sorry about the threats." Working at Checkflight never failed to be embarrassing.

When the mechanic left with our airplane, The Co and I ended up with all the work in a giant pile on the ramp. Now we had nothing to do but sit down on the pile to wait.

The Co fell asleep quickly. I tried to catch a nap, but found it tough with the constant roar of jet engines around us.

I sat there watching planes take-off and land for a few hours until, finally, our backup arrived.

Rick was the captain that dispatch had sent down along with a copilot to finish the route, and he didn't seem a bit upset that he had been woken up to fly. In fact, he seemed happy. The only thing Rick cared about was girls, and there was a cute girl who worked in the airport here in Charlotte that he wanted to hit on.

Girls were definitely Rick's weakness, and his aviation record had been tarnished because of it. A couple years ago Rick almost landed a plane gear up because he was trying to hit on a female air traffic controller over the radio. He realized the gear was up, and snapped out of his trance when the props hit the runway, q-tipping them. Rick acted quick by throwing the throttles forward; performing a balked landing. He came back around and safely landed the plane with the gear down, but the damage to the props, and his reputation, had already been done. The controller that he had been hitting on witnessed the whole thing from the tower. Rick didn't get a date.

Ricks dreams of working for a major airline were also shattered that day. Since then he's been turned down for several jobs because of that incident. But, if you ask him, he'll tell you different. Rick now claims that he is no longer interested in flying for a major airline because he can't stand their security standards. "The TSA took my weed-whacker away," he once told me, "I didn't even have any gas in it. The gas can was in my checked baggage."

Prior to Rick telling me this, I'd flown as a passenger out of Atlanta's Hartsfield-Jackson Airport. At the TSA security checkpoint, there is a display case containing, what I'd assumed to be, items that have been confiscated from passengers, including: weed-whackers, chain-saws, gas-edger's, hedge-trimmers, several gas cans, and other lawn equipment. When I first saw this, I laughed about it, thinking, *who tried to bring these things on the plane.*

Then Rick told me the story about the weed-whacker confiscation, and it dawned on me that; *Rick is originally from Atlanta.* So, I mentioned the display case, to which he replied; "Yeah, that's all my shit."

"Why the hell did you want to bring a weed-whacker on an airplane?" I asked.

His response, "you never know when you might need one."

Why Rick would want to bring his weed-whacker with him when he travels, I have no idea. It is true that the security processes for cargo flights are much more lackadaisical than passenger flights, and in most cases non-existent. In fact, I'm pretty sure people could ship packages on Checkflight without even paying for it. We have no screening process for packages, and the pilots have no information about what packages are supposed to be on their planes. If someone shows up to the airport, claiming to be a courier, and hands me a package, it goes on the plane. Even if I called dispatch, they are so confused most of the time that they don't know what is supposed to be shipping either. The time it would take them to check on a single package would cause us delays, possibly causing deadlines to be missed. So, their response is always; take the package.

On Checkflight, Rick is free to bring his weed-whackers and gasoline wherever he pleases.

Rick and I were the last remaining pilots left at Checkflight that were here before the purge.

Two years ago, when it became clear that the business of hauling checks was soon to become a thing of the past, The Chief made his first attempt at saving this company. While some of our competitors saw the need to look for other types of cargo to fly, to carry their airlines into the future. The Chief felt the best means of assuring our survival was to scrape up what little check business was left and cut costs.

"We'll be the cheapest airline in the business." He had said, and his first means of cost cutting was doing away with expensive employees.

There had been many freight captains at Checkflight that had been with the company for years, some of which had been here since the beginning, and their salaries reflected their tenure. These highly experienced freight dogs were the captains that I had the honor to fly with the first two years I worked here, when I was a first officer*. The

Chief quickly did away with all of them, replacing them with anyone who would fly for cheap. This is how sub-grade pilots such as The Co and Chip came to work here.

*- Co-pilot is an archaic term that is no longer used in aviation. The second-in-command is now referred to as the First Officer, reflecting modern beliefs that a flight crew is a team. However, I do not consider my current co-pilots, The Co and Chip, to be worthy of being called First Officers due to the fact that I would probably, no definitely, be better off without them.

The Purge was not just limited to the pilot group. The qualified mechanics and dispatchers that we used to have were let go as well, making it possible for people like Tony and Karen to find employment here. Barbara, who was once a qualified flight dispatcher, was allowed to stay, due to the fact that she no longer had any concept of what she was supposed to be paid these days. The downside to this being, that she also no longer had any concept of how to perform a flight dispatchers' duties anymore either, making her mostly useless. But she filled the FAA's requirement for having a dispatcher on duty, and that was all The Chief cared about.

At the time of the purge, I had a chance to leave Checkflight. Regrettably I choose to stay because it gave me the opportunity to upgrade to captain. There were other jobs available back then, at better companies, but I thought I'd stick it out here for a bit to gain some captain time in my logbook. What a mistake. These days I'd give anything to go back in time and get out when I had the chance.

Rick was feeling the frustration of being stuck here just the same as I was, the big difference between the two of us being the scar on his record. However, Rick was a good guy, who messed up once, and was now paying for it. Lately though, I think Rick's frustrations were really beginning to get to him. He was having trouble coming to terms with the fact that he didn't have much of a future in aviation, and his behavior was becoming a little batty.

"What it be like man?" Rick asked me, as he jumped off the wing of the plane. He was wearing a white pilot's shirt, with a black tie and epaulets, but the sleeves were cut off.

This raised two important questions, the first being; "why are you wearing a uniform?" Freight Dogs don't wear uniforms. This was obviously unacceptable attire.

"Gotta look good for the ladies." Rick responded.

Okay, I thought. *You'd look better in a Checkflight hoodie, like the rest of us wear.*

And, my second question ... "Where's your sleeves?"

"Oh, I'm a juice-head now." Rick said.

I saw Rick's co-pilot snicker in the background, it looked like he had already gotten an earful of this on the way over.

"A what?" I asked.

"A juice-head," Rick said, "I got a sore throat, so I went to the doctor and he gave me some steroids. I'm so ripped now, that I had to cut the sleeves off all my shirts. The guns just couldn't be contained, ya know."

Ripped is not the word I would use to describe Rick's physic, chubby I think is a better choice. His "guns" were not any different from the last time I saw him, and I'm pretty sure that the type of steroids that a doctor would give him for a sore throat were not the same kind that a body builder would use.

"Yeah man, you look like a gorilla." I said.

"I know, right." He said, "It's ridiculous. I'm huge."

"Awesome, well, here's the work." I said, pointing down to the giant pile I was sitting on. The Co was asleep on the ramp next to the pile of work; he had been using a bag of checks as a pillow.

I threw a box at him. "Wake up," I yelled, "let's go to the hotel!"

I helped Rick and his co-pilot load their plane while The Co watched. At this point, the work was beyond late but Rick didn't seem to be in a hurry. After we loaded the plane, he spent thirty minutes in the airport hitting on some girl at the front desk before departing. By this point, the customers must have been furious that the cargo had not yet arrived. I could only imagine what they were saying to Barbara right now, and I'm sure they were in no mood to talk about her poop.

Since The Co and I were finally done for the day, it was time to go to the hotel that Barbara had booked for us to get some sleep.

We ran into another delay, though. We had to rely on the hotel's shuttle bus to pick us up at the airport, and the shuttle driver had no idea where we were.

When you tell people that you're "at the airport," they assume you mean the terminal where all the passengers go. But we weren't at the terminal. We were at an FBO, on the other side of the airport.

An FBO or Fixed Base Operator is a commercial operator supplying fuel, coffee, maintenance, computers for flight planning or downloading porn, hangars, de-ice, and other services at an airport. The better ones have free popcorn and cookies.

Freight Dogs often refer to FBO's as "home" because many of us, that can't afford to pay rent on an apartment, live in FBO crew lounges, and survive on a diet of whatever free snacks they're offering.

The airport is a big place with many more buildings than just the terminal, but most people don't know this. I tried to explain to the shuttle driver how to get to where we were, but he wouldn't listen.

He just kept asking me which terminal we were at. I tried several times to give him directions, but I couldn't get through to him. Finally, I had to tell him that we were not at the airport but we were near the airport. Then he listened to my directions.

It was late afternoon by the time I got to my hotel room. Finally, I went to sleep.

- 5 -
It's Raining Checks

I woke up in my hotel room to my phone ringing off the hook. With the heavy curtains drawn it was pitch dark in the room, though glancing at the alarm clock on the nightstand, I saw that it was early evening. It had only been a few hours since The Co and I had finally gone to bed. I picked up my phone to check the caller ID. It was dispatch, so I decided not to answer it.

Why the hell are they calling? Don't they know I'm sleeping?

A few minutes later the phone started ringing again; this time it was The Chief. I was already up now, and figuring he was just calling to find out what had happened this morning with the oil leak, I answered.

"Hello."

"We've got another route for you to do," he said. "How quick can you get to the airport?"

"What? I'm sleeping. I just got to bed a couple hours ago."

"But you went off duty at seven o'clock this morning. That was ten hours ago, correct?"

Just like our maximum duty time, we also have a minimum rest time, which was ten hours. *And, he really shouldn't be calling me during my*

81

rest!

"No," I said, "I was scheduled to go off duty at seven, but I flew the route you wanted me to, which took me way past seven, but you know about that. Plus, we had a mechanical problem and had to wait for backup."

"Yeah, I know about all that," he said, "but I had dispatch check you out at seven anyway, to make sure everything looked legit on paper. So, if you were off duty at seven, then you've got your ten hours of rest and should be able to go back on duty now."

"But I didn't go off duty at seven. I was barely starting at seven. I've only been at the hotel sleeping for a couple hours now, so I haven't got my ten hours of rest."

"Well, that's not what the computer says."

"That's because you set it up that way!" I was getting mad now. "I don't care what your computer says! It says what you want it to say, so you can abuse us!"

"Just so I'm clear here, are you refusing a duty assignment even though the computer clearly shows that you have had enough rest?"

God damn it, I thought, *there's no way out of this.* "No, I'm not refusing an assignment. I'll wake The Co up, and we'll get to the airport."

"Thank you."

"Is the plane fixed?"

"Yes, they've got it all done."

"Bye," I said, and hung up. *Asshole.*

I got my stuff packed and then went down to The Co's room so I could wake him up. But, after several minutes of pounding on his door without him answering, I gave up.

I went down to the lobby to see if they could open The Co's door, so I could blast him out of bed with the fire-hose or something.

But, as I walked through the lobby, I spotted The Co sitting at the bar. I should have known he'd be here.

"We have to go," I said, as I approached him.

"What?" he questioned, taking a sip from his gin and tonic, "but I just ordered another round."

"Well, cancel it. The Chief just called. We've got to fly, so pay your tab and let's go."

"Oh, alright." The Co said. He finished his drink, paid his tab, and got his things from his room.

The guy at the front desk seemed surprised to hear that we were checking out so soon. "Didn't you guys just check in like two hours ago?" he asked.

"Yup," I said, "work, you know."

"I hear ya. The shuttle's outside, he'll take you to the airport."

"Thanks."

I made sure to tell the shuttle driver that we were not going to the airport, but we were going to a place that was near the airport. He listened to my directions.

When we pulled up in front of the FBO where our plane was parked, the shuttle driver asked, "So what is this place?"

"The airport," I said, figuring now that we were here it was safe to tell him that.

"No, this isn't the airport; the airport is that way," he said, pointing in the general direction of the terminal.

"Yeah, you're right. I don't know what this place is." I gave up.

When we got to our airplane, I was surprised to find that the engine had been replaced. Or, at least that's what the maintenance log said. Usually it takes days to perform an engine change. Somehow, they pulled this off in a couple hours. Or maybe they just fixed the oil leak and claimed to have replaced the engine. With Tony in charge you never could tell.

I fired up both engines, and they seemed to be running well. There was one problem though. All of the temperature and pressure gauges for the left engine, the one that had been replaced, were not working. My first instinct was to check the circuit breakers to see if the one for the engine gauges had popped. It hadn't. I wonder if they forgot to hook up the sensors or if they left them unhooked on purpose because the engine was not running within limits.

Oh well, what you don't know can't hurt you. The engine seemed to be running okay.

I called dispatch to find out exactly what they needed us to do. Not to my surprise, the route we were going to fly would take us through the night and into the morning. Again.

I was tired last night, now I'd gotten just two hours of sleep and I had to do this again. I was pissed. Anytime pilots have to fly on no sleep, mistakes are bound to be made, and when you flew with The Co the chances of making a mistake increased ten-fold.

The night seemed to drag on forever. At every stop we made, I drank a cup of coffee and then another. Then I'd get another cup for the road. I faded in and out of sleep the entire night. At one point, I fell asleep while on final approach into Teterboro. I woke up just as we were crossing the threshold. "Oh shit!" I yelled, as I threw the gear down just seconds before impacting the runway. The Co was sound asleep. I held the plane off the runway, and quickly made sure we were cleared to land. "Teterboro Tower confirm Checkflight 101 is cleared to land?"

"Yes, 101, I've already confirmed that for you twice already, you're cleared to land on runway one-niner."

I must have dosed off and woke up a few times since we'd been on final, each time asking for another landing clearance.

"Thanks, cleared to land one-nine," I said, then let the wheels touch down.

As we cleared the runway the tower controller said, "Checkflight 101 taxi to the ramp, this frequency."

"Checkflight 101 taxi to the ramp with you," I read back.

"Is everything alright with you guys?" The tower controller asked. "You asked if you were cleared to land three times after you had already been cleared, and it looked like you didn't put your gear down until very short final."

"We're good," I responded, and left it at that.

On the next leg, it was early morning now, and the sun was rising. This was our second-to-last flight for the day, a long stretch from Teterboro to Cleveland. We'd been battling headwinds the whole way, but after Cleveland, it was just a quick hop back to our home base in nowhere Ohio.

I started to feel some relief in the knowledge that we'd be home soon, but remembering the events of yesterday, I knew there was still plenty of time for something to go wrong. I was bored, and The Co and I had run out of things to talk about hours ago. I decided to try and pry him for some dirt.

That night I hung out with The Co's friends back in his hometown, one of his friends hinted at an incident in which The Co woke up in some guy's bed. I was never able to get the full story, as The Co kept saying "We're not going to speak about that," and made his friend change the subject.

I started pestering him to spill it. We had nothing else to do, and a good embarrassing story seemed like just the thing to keep me awake.

"So, this waking up in some guy's bed, let's hear it."

"No way," The Co said. "I told you that story was never to be spoken of again."

"Come on, man," I begged. "I'm falling asleep here. Besides, who else am I going to tell?"

"No!"

"Man, I'm gonna get it out of you eventually, you might as well tell me now."

"Fine, I'll tell you," he caved. "But you better not repeat it."

"I won't, promise."

"Well, nothing really happened. It's not that big a deal. I went out drinking one night, and, afterwards, I crashed at a buddy's house. The guy lived with his dad, and it was close to the bar we were at; I didn't want to drive home. My license was not technically valid at the time, so it seemed like a good idea to sleep there and go home in the morning."

I laughed, "was this the suspension from crashing into the house?"

"No, this was a different suspension."

"How many have there been?"

"Several——. Anyway, I passed out on the couch. But at some point, I must have gotten up and walked into the dad's bedroom and got in bed with him."

"Well, I could guess that much. Is that it?"

"Well, I took my clothes off before getting in bed. I must've been hot."

"Are you serious?" I laughed.

"Very serious. But I don't remember it at all." He cracked a smile and shrugged his shoulders.

"The guy didn't wake up?"

"I guess he slept through it. In the morning, I opened my eyes and there I was face to face with this guy I've never seen before. We just laid there staring at each other not speaking a word for what seemed like an eternity, then I just got up and left."

"And your clothes?"

"I picked them up on my way out."

"Holy shit! Have you seen this guy since?"

"No way, never been back, and that was like eight years ago."

I was dying laughing and definitely wide awake at this point. "Yeah, but those days of getting into ridiculous situations are behind you, right?"

The Co laughed. "Well, hopefully that doesn't happen again."

Just then Cleveland Center interrupted. "Checkflight 101 contact Cleveland Approach on one-two-five point three-five."

"Checkflight 101, twenty-five thirty-five, see ya." I answered.

It was time to descend into Cleveland, and I couldn't wait to get there. I'd had four cups of coffee on the last flight in an effort to stay awake, and I needed to pee, bad. Approach control vectored us for the airport, and I was flying as fast as I could, banking hard, and descending fast.

Still thinking about The Co's story, I couldn't stop laughing. Air traffic control must've thought I was crazy because I kept cracking-up during every radio transmission.

Cleared for the visual, and turning final over Lake Erie, I chopped the throttles, banked hard left at eighty degrees, and dumped the gear.

"Hey, fly safe," The Co said.

"Why do you say that?"

"'Cause the story I just told is on the CVR*, and I don't want anybody to hear it."

*- The CVR (Cockpit Voice Recorder), also known as the black box (it's actually orange), records everything said over the cockpit intercom. The tape runs on a continuously overwriting loop, always leaving a record of the last thirty minutes of flight. If a flight crew should find themselves in an emergency situation during, or shortly following, an embarrassing conversation; it may become necessary to keep the plane airborne for up to thirty minutes before crashing to keep their conversation from becoming public record.

"Don't worry," I said. "I always fly safe."

A couple minutes later we were on the ground at Cleveland's Burke Lakefront Airport, I ran inside to use the restroom and left The Co in charge of loading the plane. The courier was already there, and this stop was just a pickup, so all The Co had to do was toss a few more bags in the plane.

Once I got back outside, The Co was already sitting in the plane.

"Ready to go?" I asked, as I climbed in.

"Yup," he said, "we're all loaded up."

Normally I would never trust any responsibility to The Co unless he was under my direct supervision, but I was beyond tired and in a hurry to get home. I assumed that he had closed all of the cargo compartments after loading them.

Wrong!

I fired the engines up, called the tower, and, in just a couple minutes, we were rolling down the runway.

About two seconds after breaking ground, the nose baggage door burst open.

"Shit!" I yelled, "Did you close that?"

"I thought I did," The Co said.

"You thought?"

"I guess it didn't latch all the way?"

The baggage door flapped wildly in the one-hundred knot plus airflow, testing the structural integrity of the hinges. There was no way we could fly home with this thing open. Once the plane got up to cruise speed, it would probably rip off. On top of that, we could lose the cargo that was in there.

"We're gonna have to go back and close this thing," I said.

The Co shrugged his shoulders, he could care less.

"Lakefront Tower, Checkflight 101; we've got a baggage door open we need to come back around," I said into the mic.

"Roger that Checkflight 101. I've got traffic on right downwind for two-four right, make left traffic for two-four left; cleared to land."

"Left traffic, two-four left; cleared to land"

I pulled the power back to keep us as slow as possible and banked the plane gently to the left, over the city. We passed over Browns Stadium and the Rock and Roll Hall of Fame as we made the turn, rolling out to parallel the runway right over the center of downtown.

Just then, a forty-pound bag of checks flew out of the nose compartment, hitting the left prop, shredding it open. Seconds later, another followed, then another, and another, until the nose compartment was empty. The sky was filled with confetti.

"Well, there goes all the work," I said, as I looked back over my shoulder at the trail of debris.

"Checkflight 101, it looks like you're losing your cargo," the control tower informed us.

"Thanks, we're aware."

When we landed, I didn't even know what to do. We had just lost a few hundred pounds of checks into the morning sky, right over a

Alex Stone

major city. I parked the airplane on the ramp, right back in the same spot we had just left. I got out without saying another word to The Co. I paced around on the ramp for a few minutes trying to figure out what to do.

I needed to call Checkflight and let them know what had happened, so I went inside to get away from the noise on the ramp.

As soon as I walked in the door, I looked up at the TV, and there it was on the morning news.

News reporter on TV:

> I'm standing in downtown Cleveland where it has been raining checks. That's right: raining checks; bank checks are falling out of the sky. Just minutes ago, witnesses reported seeing a small, twin-engine airplane fly over the city while debris seemed to be falling out of the airplane. No word yet on what happened here as crowds of onlookers are gathering to watch checks fall from the sky.

Wow, they picked up the story quick, I thought. People in the airport were all looking at me then back at the TV. The Co walked up next to me, watching the news report, and he started laughing.

"It's a little bit funny, don't you think?" he said.

"I doubt The Chief will find it funny," I said, "and I'm sure the customer won't either."

"Oh well, you win some, you lose some."

"Are you kidding me? This is a disaster! I wouldn't be surprised if FEMA shows up and starts throwing down sand bags!"

"Don't be so dramatic. It's not that bad."

"Not that bad? We might get investigated for this, I mean we've got to report it. It's already on the news!"

We had the attention of everyone in the room now. Everyone was looking at the TV then staring at us as we argued.

This is what happens anytime I delegate any kind of responsibility to The Co. He screws it up, and now we looked like asses on national television.

If this was already on TV, I needed to call dispatch quick. They would have to be the one to break the news to the customer. The banks want to know about any delays with their work. If they saw this on TV before hearing from us, they'd be pretty upset. Not to mention the fact that the checks may be raining down on the front steps of the very banks that just shipped them.

The phone rang.

"Dispatch, this is Barbara," she answered.

"Hi Barbara, this is 101; we had a little problem." I explained to her what had happened.

"You're a bunch of idiots! Take me to the bathroom, and then I'm coming back here to take over!"

"Barbara, I can't take you to the bathroom. I'm in Cleveland. Did you hear what I said about losing the work?"

"No, you idiot! I'm eliminating!"

"Barbara, did you say you're eliminating?"

"Yes, stupid; I'm eliminating! You're a bunch of idiots."

"Alright Barbara, I'm gonna let you go then." I hung up. She was obviously completely out of her mind this morning and had no idea what I was talking about. We had to call The Chief.

"What did she say? Was she pissed?" The Co asked.

"Barbara's off her rocker," I said. "We've gotta call The Chief, and I think you should call. He likes you better for some reason, and, technically, this is all your fault."

"Fine, I'll do it," The Co said as he started to dial.

For some reason, The Co got away with everything. The Chief would never fire him no matter what he did. Anyone else would be canned for this, but I knew that The Co would get off scot-free.

Not to my surprise, when The Co got off the phone with The Chief, he said, "He thinks it's your fault."

But, never-the-less I was upset by this. "What? *My* fault? You're the one who was supposed to close the cargo doors; that was your only responsibility!"

"Yeah, but you're the PIC," The Co said, "so technically you're responsible."

Typical, I thought, *always blame the PIC.*

The PIC or Pilot in Command is responsible for the safety of the flight. I was the PIC; this meant I was responsible. Even though my copilot was so worthless that he couldn't even manage to close the baggage door properly after loading the cargo, which was literally the only responsibility he'd had the whole day, I still got blamed for it.

"Well, what did The Chief want us to do?" I asked.

"He said don't talk to the press and come home."

"Well then, let's get out of here."

The news report continued as we headed for the door.

> *We're getting word now that the small cargo plane reportedly took off from Cleveland's Burke Lakefront Airport and had a cargo compartment open in flight. The aircraft was a twin-engine cargo plane operated by Checkflight Airlines. The flight reportedly landed safely back at Burke Lakefront Airport a few minutes later. Checkflight operates flights for several local banks. We are attempting to contact the company for a statement.*

A crowd was gathering outside the airport fence near where our plane was parked. I closed the nose baggage door that had still been hanging open. *At least the hinges held.* News cameras filmed me as I climbed into the plane.

The Co decided to put on a show for the cameras. He jumped up on the wing facing the crowd, waved and took a bow.

"Hey, dumb ass, get in the plane," I said. "You know that's gonna be on the news."

"I don't care," The Co responded, and in one of the grandest displays of unwarranted showmanship I'd ever seen; The Co threw his arms towards the sky, tilted his head back forming some sort of victory stance, and screamed, "I love you Cleveland!"

The crowd erupted in applause, and I swear to god I saw somebody shoot a bottle rocket out of a beer bottle.

Back at our home base, however, The Chief was in no celebratory mood. He had been standing there on the ramp with his arms crossed, waiting for us. "Boy, you put on quite a show," he said, as we stepped out of the plane.

"Talk to him," I said, pointing at The Co.

The Chief glared at me. He stuck his finger in my face, and angrily said, "No, I'm talking to you! I'm getting sick of you screwing up every day. Yesterday, you didn't finish the run. Today, you took off with a baggage door open—"

"Hey!" I screamed back at him. "Your plane broke down yesterday, because it's not maintained properly! And, the door came open because The Co didn't shut it! If you want things to get done, you need to do your part … Give me a plane that's actually airworthy, and a crew that is capable of doing their job, and maybe things would go a little smoother around here." I turned to The Co, "Sorry Co, but as a crew member, you suck."

The Co looked up in confusion. "Huh? I wasn't listening."

"Never mind." I said.

The Chief stared at me for a moment, grinding his teeth. "Well, I've got a whole bunch of paperwork for you to do," He said, apparently unable to find a comeback.

"Great. Well, let's get it over with."

Of course, The Co got to go home, but, because I was the PIC, I had to stay and fill out pages upon pages of paperwork for the next three hours.

I had to provide detailed accounts of the incidents of the last two nights. Basically, all of it amounted to: me taking responsibility for everything that's gone wrong. As he handed me the stack of papers, The Chief even said, "Don't you dare try to blame any of this on anyone but yourself!"

"Oh, I wouldn't dream of it." I said. The veins in my forehead were swelling with anger. "I'm just so sorry I'm ruining the reputation of your great company."

I went to the pilot's lounge and cleared the cracker crumbs off one of the recliners so I could sit down, and I got to work on the ridiculous paperwork.

"How could this incident be prevented in the future?" One of the forms asked. "By properly supervising the duties of my co-pilot, during cargo loading operations," I wrote. What a bunch of bullshit. I wanted to write "I QUIT," right across the front of every page, but I knew I couldn't. Like it or not, I was trapped at Checkflight, there was nowhere else for me to go. Playing The Chiefs game was the only option I had.

By the end of it, I was so tired that I was drooling on the forms. I could barely even read my own writing anymore.

When I finally finished, I threw the papers on The Chief's desk.

"Thanks, have a good weekend." He said, like a smart ass.

"Adios," I said, with a smile. With all the crap that had gone on the last two nights, I had almost forgotten that it was Friday. It couldn't have come at a better time.

- 6 -
I've Got Glitter on My Face

When you work the night shift, seeing the sun shine becomes a luxury. I usually only saw the sun for a few minutes a day, before going to sleep in the morning. In the winter, it became worse as the days got shorter and the nights got longer. I slept through what little sunshine there was.

For freight dogs, weekends off are not the same as they are for the nine-to-five people. Even on my days off, I slept through the day and I'd be up at night. This results in very little contact with the outside world. Basically, the only people I knew anymore were the pilots I worked with, a bunch of weird couriers, and whatever other creepy crawlers were up late at night.

A bunch of the pilots usually went out on Saturday nights, and we'd stay out way past when the rest of the bar hoppers go to sleep, because when the bar closes at three a.m. it's the middle of the day for us. So, what's open after three a.m.? Strip clubs.

Everyone met over at my apartment at eight p.m. I had just eaten breakfast and gotten dressed for the day. We were driving down to Columbus because there was nothing open around here, in nowhere

Ohio, late at night.

The Co and Rick were already here, and we were waiting for Chip to show up. Now, Chip didn't usually hang out with us. In fact, this would be the first time. He was newly single after his second wife left him, so, out of pity, we invited him to come along.

Rick was ready to do some bird doggin', and that's all he was talking about.

Bird doggin' means, when you see a good-looking girl, you go on point like a German Shorthair Pointer would when it found a pheasant. Rick basically lived his life around bird doggin', and Saturday night was bird doggin' night.

"You ready to do some bird doggin'?" he asked me.

To which I asked him, "Can you bird dog without sleeves?" Rick was wearing a red striped button up shirt, tucked in, negative sleeves.

"You can definitely bird dog sans sleeves," he said. "No sleeve's is the best way to bird dog, in fact; if I ever become a millionaire, I'm never wearing sleeves again."

"That's what you would do if you were a millionaire; cut your sleeves off? I don't think you have to be a millionaire to macro-made your shirts. I mean, you're not wearing sleeves now and you're definitely not a millionaire."

"Yeah, but then I could have sleeveless shirts custom tailored."

Is he serious? I paused for a second, trying to comprehend Rick's dream of; having a tailor chop his sleeves off.

The Co poked his head out from my kitchen where he had had been rifling through the cabinets, "Got anything we can take shots of?" he asked.

"There's some Krupnik in the cabinet above the fridge." I said.

The Co opened the cabinet, upon finding the bottle he rejoiced, "Sweet!"

"Be careful with that stuff though, it'll rot your gut out." I warned him.

The Co examined the bottle. "What is this stuff anyway?"

"It's Polish liquor."

"Is it any good?"

I took the bottle from him. "Well they've been making it since eighteen forty-six," I said, pointing to the label, "you figure if it wasn't good, they'd have gone out of business by now."

I handed the bottle back to The Co. "Good enough for me. You want some?" he asked.

"Not yet, I'm still waiting for my breakfast to settle."

"Come on." The Co begged.

"Fine— one." I gave in.

"Rick?"

"Sure," Rick said.

The Co poured three shots of the caramel colored alcohol; we each grabbed one off the counter.

"To bird doggin'," Rick toasted.

"To more shots," The Co added, and we drank.

When Chip finally got to my apartment, he was already drunk. I mean sloppy drunk. I guess he had been nervous about going out and went a little overboard "taking the edge off."

"How'd you get here?" I asked him as he propped himself up by the kitchen counter to keep from falling.

"I drove," he said, already slurring his speech. He held his hands up like he was motioning a steering wheel, but he had his two index fingers pointing straight up as he said, "in between the lines."

"Alright," I said, "well, glad you made it here safely. Let's get going."

We walked out to the parking lot towards Rick's car. I

immediately noticed that Chip's car was parked crookedly, not even close to being in a parking spot, and the passenger side was all smashed up. I've seen his car in the parking lot at work before, and I don't remember it being damaged.

"Hey, what happened to your car, man?" I asked him.

"I don't know," he said. "What's wrong with it?"

"It's all smashed up on the passenger side." I pointed to the damage.

"Oh, I think I hit something on the way over."

"Holy shit!" Rick yelled, seeing the damage for himself, "you think you hit something? What did you hit? Your car is practically totaled!"

"I don't know," Chip said confused. "Is it bad? 'Cause I can't see it."

"It's pretty freaking smashed up," I said.

"Yeah," Rick added, "it's bad."

"Oh, it'll be fine," Chip said, obviously too wasted to grasp the situation.

"If you say so," I said.

The Co jumped in, impatiently, "Who cares, let's go. It's not a big deal. Cars get smashed up all the time."

"Damn, impatient!" I said. "We're going."

We all piled into Rick's car, which was quite uncomfortable because we had to share the back seat with his roto-tiller.

"Why do you have this?" I asked Rick, referring to the large piece of machinery that crowded the car.

"It's my roto-tiller." Rick responded.

"Yeah, I know, but why do you have it? What are you roto-tilling? You live in an apartment."

"Well, nothing right now," Rick said, "but someday..."

Never mind. I let it go.

I peered over the top of the roto-tiller at Chip. He was slumped forward in his seat, with his eyes closed. I started to think that inviting him may have been a bad idea. This guy never left his house except to go to work, and had no idea how to act in public. He had already drank more than he probably should all night and wrecked his car, and it was only eight o'clock. We had a long night ahead of us, and I didn't know if he could handle it.

Chip remained silently slumped over for the first few minutes of the drive, till Rick started accelerating down the expressway on-ramp.

Chip picked his head up, and looked out the window. "Where are we going?" He blurted out. I think the sight of the expressway scared him.

"Columbus," I answered.

"Oh, the big city; I've never been," Chip said, and then asked "is it safe to go there?"

I wouldn't worry about it, Chip," I assured him. "Just relax; we've got a long drive."

Chip leaned his head forward against the back of Rick's seat. He sat like that for most of the drive, except for the two times he requested that we pull over so he could puke.

The puke stops added time to the drive, but eventually we made it to Columbus. We parked the car and walked to a bar in the Arena District.

When we got a table at the bar, Rick started going over the order of "The Plan" for the night. He does this every week; I don't know if he thought we'd forget or he just liked to remind us.

"Alright, Plan A is find hot chicks," Rick said, "Plan B is ugly chicks, and Plan C is the strip club. Got it?"

"We know, we know," The Co said, impatiently. "You tell us

every week. Now who wants shots?"

The Co could care less about the plan; his only concern was alcohol. He returned a few minutes later with a huge tray that had two beers for each of us, a round of tequila shots, and a round of Jaeger Bombs.

We all took the tequila shots first. When Chip finished his he slammed the glass on the table and yelled, "I'm drunk!" We all stared at him as did many other people who were sitting around us. Seconds later his face went slack, and he dropped off his bar stool like a sack of potatoes.

We had the attention of everyone in the bar now, even the bartenders were staring at us, probably wondering if they should kick us out.

"God damn it," The Co said. "Are we going to have to babysit him all night?"

"Oh, you're one to talk," I shot back. "Nobody's ever had to babysit you?"

"Touché."

"I'll take him to the bathroom and put him in a stall for now," Rick said, while hopping off his bar stool.

"Good idea." I agreed. "You need help?"

"No, I got it."

Rick reached down and grabbed Chip's arms. Everyone in the bar watched as Rick dragged Chip's limp body across the floor, towards the bathroom.

Once the bathroom door closed, show was over, and everyone went back to their business. The Co and I sat there sipping our beers. Actually, The Co was slamming his. "You better not be the next one to get dragged off." I warned him.

"Well, I can't promise anything." The Co reassured me.

I looked over at four girls, who had just walked into the bar. They walked right passed us, but as they passed our table, one of them did a double take on The Co. "Did you see that?" I asked.

"See what?" The Co had obviously missed it.

The girls all sat down at a table on the other side of the bar, but the one girl kept looking over.

"I think she likes you," I said, nodding my head in the girl's direction.

"You think?" The Co asked, taking another chug of his beer.

"Well she keeps checking you out."

The girl got up, and walked towards us. "Here she comes."

The girl approached The Co and asked, "Hey, did I see you on TV yesterday?"

"Maybe," The Co answered, smiling shyly.

"Yeah," the girl said, "you were on TV. You're the guy that took a bow on the airplane wing."

"Yeah," The Co said, "that was us," pointing to me.

The girl looked at me. "Yeah, I saw you too. That was hilarious! They were playing that clip on CNN all day. What happened?"

"Ask him," I said, pointing to The Co.

"Oh, it was nothing," The Co said. "We just had a problem with our airplane, and we landed safely."

The Co was taking a bet that this girl was stupid, because if she had actually paid attention to the news, she would know that what had happened was all our fault. The news networks had been bashing us and Checkflight for the last twenty-four hours. I had been worried that people might recognize us tonight.

"Wow, so you guys are like heroes?"

"Well, I don't like being called a hero but...," The Co said, obviously loving his new-found fame.

"That's, like, so amazing, were you scared?"

"Not really," he answered.

"I would be so scared," she said.

"It's just a normal day for us." That was actually the first thing he said that was honest. On a normal day, with all the stuff we're put through, we should be considered heroes. But what happened yesterday was all the result of The Co's incompetence. It sure was working out for him today though.

"Wow, that's amazing. I'm gonna go get my friends," she said, pointing towards her table, "I'll be right back."

"Okay."

As soon as she walked away, I said, "She's perfect for you."

"You think?" The Co asked, as he put the finishing touches on his second beer, and grabbed one of Chips.

"Well, she's the only person in the world who would consider you to be a hero."

"Ha-ha smartass."

"Hey, I'm just saying."

This was just too funny. The Co was the last person on earth that anyone would call a hero. If anything, I should be considered a hero for putting up with him every day. Some days, I feel like I deserve to meet the president because of the crap I put up with.

I often thought that if I had the same attitude as The Co, we would both just get in the plane and sit there. Neither of us would do anything, the plane would never get started, we wouldn't fly, and the cargo would never be delivered.

I wasn't even sure if he even knew how to fly. I'd never seen him fly, and he'd been my co-pilot for two years. Every time I asked him if he wanted to fly a leg, he said no, so I just quit asking.

Rick came back from helping Chip to the bathroom.

"You won't believe it!" I said. "This girl came over here and she thinks The Co is a hero!"

"Well, where'd she go?" Rick asked.

"She said she's getting her friends."

"Are her friends hot?"

"They're pretty good looking. They're right over there." I pointed to them.

"Well, let's bird dog' em!"

"Shots?" The Co jumped in.

"Alright," Rick said, "let's do these Jaeger Bombs, then we're bird doggin' those girls."

We took the Jaeger Bombs, then sent The Co over to bring the girls back.

"How's Chip?" I asked Rick.

"Oh, he's in there puking," Rick said. "I'll check on him every once in a while. What is wrong with that guy? I think we should revoke his hanging out privileges."

This was Chip's first night out with us, and already, his "hanging out privileges" were in jeopardy.

"He's been having a rough time lately," I said. "He's had two marriages fail this year. But I don't think he can handle going out. Especially not with us. Let's not give him any more shots, or he's gonna be sick all night."

"Agreed."

The Co came back with the whole group of girls. Before they could even sit down, Rick grabbed one of the girls, whispered something in her ear, and the two of them were gone. Within a minute, I spotted Rick and his girl making out on the other side of the bar. *I guess you can bird dog without sleeves.*

"Damn, that guy is straight business," I announced to no one in particular, "He doesn't mess around at all."

We hung out with those girls until the bar closed. Every once in a while, The Co would spring up and say "Shots?" Chip even came out of the bathroom after a while, though all he did was sit at the table with face down. He looked miserable. The girl I had been talking to kept asking if he was okay.

"Yeah, he doesn't go out much," I said.

"Awe, poor guy, he looks so sad."

When last call was made, the girls started hinting that they'd like us to come with them to an after-party. "We're going to a house party afterwards," one of them said. "You guys want to come with?"

Rick and I both agreed that the house party sounded like a good idea. Chip could care less. But, when the girl who was with The Co asked him if he wanted to go to the house party, he stated matter-of-factly, "No, we're not going to any house party. We're going to the strip club."

The girls stared at The Co in disgust. "Uhh, alright," the girl The Co had been talking to said.

"What the hell is wrong with you?" Rick questioned. His face was turning red.

"I don't want to go to a house party," The Co said. "We're going to the strip club."

Rick pulled The Co aside. "Dude, that girl is all over you; let's go to the house party."

"I don't care. Our plan was to go to the strip club."

"No! Plan A is to go home with these girls, Plan C is the strip club. You're skipping ahead. Now tell them that we're going with them!" Rick was getting seriously pissed.

The Co turned back towards the girls, with a big stupid smile on his face, he politely said, "Sorry, but we're going to the strip club."

The girls left after that, and Rick was furious. "Goddamn it!" He screamed, and slammed his beer bottle on the floor, shattering it.

Things got heated, quick. The two of them were in each other's face. "You're fucking up my bird doggin'!" Rick spit his words in The Co's face.

A bartender started to intervene, "You guys gotta go." He said, "Now!"

"Let's go." I said. "You guys are causing a scene." I had to pull The Co and Rick apart.

"Fine!" Rick said. He backed off, and calmed down a bit, but was still very frustrated. "Sorry, just a little roid-rage, let's go to the strip club."

When we got to the strip club, The Co couldn't have been more excited. Rick was starting to get over the fight, and he was smiling again. "Is this place any good?" He asked.

"Well, it's no Sauget," The Co informed him. "But, it's pretty good."

The Co is a connoisseur of strip clubs, and Sauget, Illinois (near St. Louis) is his Mecca. Sauget (pronounced saw-ZHAY) a town known for pollution, lawlessness, and the Ballet du Sauget is considered by some to be the strip club capitol of the world. It's a running joke amongst freight dogs that any plane that fly's to St. Louis, returns covered in glitter.

We walked into the lobby, and there was a line to get in. I guessed we weren't the only ones that came here when the bars close.

After about fifteen minutes of waiting, Chip started dancing around like he had to pee.

"Chip, settle down," I said. "You look like a crazy person."

"I gotta go," he said, rocking back and forth.

"Well there's nowhere to go here; you have to wait until we get inside."

"Damn," Chip said, looking towards the front of the line. "Do we have to pay to get in?"

"Yup, there's a cover."

"Do they take credit cards?" He asked, now hopping up and down on one leg.

"No, it's cash only, but there's an ATM over there." I pointed to an ATM a little ways down the hallway.

"I'm gonna go get cash."

"We'll be here."

Chip walked down the hall to use the ATM. I watched him as he danced around in front of it while he waited for his cash to dispense. Then, in a panic, Chip squeezed in between the ATM and the wall, unzipped his pants, and started peeing on the floor behind the ATM.

"Oh, shit!" I quickly got Rick's attention. "He's pissing behind the ATM."

"Holy shit!" Rick said, "he's gonna get us kicked out of here."

"He's gonna get his ass beat by a bouncer is what's going to happen," I said, as I looked around to see if any of the bouncers had noticed. None of them were looking that way, but I started to think the rest of us should make a run for it. Best case scenario was Chip was going to jail.

The ATM was spitting out Chip's cash into the tray while he stood there, still pissing on the floor for what seemed like an eternity. Amazingly, no one was taking notice.

When Chip finished, he walked back over and got in line with us, leaving his cash and his card in the machine.

"Are you going to get your cash?" I said pointing at the ATM. "I'm surprised with all the people in here no one swiped it yet."

"Oh, yeah." Chip went to get his cash out of the tray, but left his card in the machine.

"And your card!" I yelled to him from across the room.

"Huh?" He questioned, while walking towards us.

"Your card is still in the machine, dumbass!"

"Oh." Chip turned around, and went back to the ATM to retrieve his card.

"You're a freakin' idiot," I said to him when he got back. "You pissed in the lobby of a strip club. There's like ten bouncers in here who would've loved to beat your ass if they'd seen you."

"Sorry man, I had to go."

Rick was laughing, "I can't believe no one noticed. Nice job, Chip."

Within a few minutes we were inside. We got a table, near the main stage, and a waitress came by to take our drink order. "What can I get you guys?"

"Shots." The Co said. He ordered a round of tequila shots and two rounds of beers.

"Except no tequila for Chip." I spoke up. Though he did seem to be feeling a lot better at this point, giving him another shot would probably put him right back in the toilet.

No less than two minutes after taking that first round of tequila shots, The Co again suggested, "Shots?" And, again a few minutes later, "Shots?" Each time ordering another round.

Everyone was getting pretty drunk at this point. We were throwing around cash like money was no object, although we'd all probably regret this when we got our next bank statement.

The Co got a seat right in front of the stage. He kept yelling, "I

107

like your style," at every girl that was up there as he threw singles out. About every fifteen minutes, he'd come back to the table and say "Shots?" He'd take a shot, then go right back to his seat in front of the stage.

Even Chip seemed to be having a good time at this point. For the first time tonight, he didn't look like warmed over shit. He was drinking beers, but we kept him away from the hard alcohol. One girl kept coming back to him, sitting down and talking. I think he must've gotten twenty lap dances from her. Only they weren't actually lap dances, just talking.

"I think I love her," Chip told me, nodding towards the stripper he'd been talking to. She was giving a lap dance to a guy a few tables away. "She really wants to talk to me, and we've got a lot in common."

Oh, crap, here we go. "Just remember she's just doing that for the tips," I warned him.

Chip didn't seem to care though; he liked the attention. He must've made twenty-some trips to the ATM to get more cash, and I have no idea how much he was taking out each time. Every time I looked over at Chip that girl was sitting on his lap, talking to him, and every few minutes he'd hand her money.

But when it came time to leave Chip seemed upset again. "Let's go," he said, frowning like someone stole his bicycle.

"What, you want to leave? I thought you were in love?" It was hard not to crack a smile while saying this.

"Well, I thought that she really liked me, but I asked for her phone number, and she wouldn't give it to me."

"Cheer up man, there will be others."

It was seven a.m. when we left the strip club, and the Sunday morning church crowd was already out and about. On the way home, we stopped at the grocery store to get more beer, and some food to grill out. Chip had fallen asleep in the car, so we left him there while we shopped.

When we got inside, Rick said he was going to get some milk.

"What?" The Co questioned. "Milk?"

"Yeah, I need milk."

"Alright," I said, "The Co and I will find stuff to grill. Come find us when you get your milk."

We picked up a case of beer, ground beef and buns for burgers, and were looking for the charcoal aisle when Rick found us.

"Do you know where the eggs are at?" Rick asked. He had milk, energy bars, and a can of protein supplement in his basket already.

"What? Are you doing your weekly shopping?" The Co asked. "This was supposed to be quick stop to grab some beer and food to grill, not a shopping trip."

"No, I'm not doing my weekly shopping. I'm just grabbing a few things."

"Is that what you eat?" I asked Rick, referring to the items in his basket.

"Yeah, I told you I'm a juice-head. That's why I need eggs."

"Well, hurry up," The Co said, throwing a bag of charcoal under the cart, "we're ready to go."

Once Rick got all his groceries together, he went to check out. As the cashier was scanning his items he was digging in his wallet.

"What are you doing? Do you not have any money? The Co was really starting to flip out; he hadn't had a drink since we left the strip club, and every second of delay greatly upset him.

"No, I've got money," Rick said, "but, I've got coupons for some of this stuff; I'm trying to find them."

"Oh my god!" The Co screamed. "Forget the coupons, just pay

for the stuff, I'm thirsty!"

Back at my apartment, I brought the grill out to the parking lot, and we fired it up. Rick and I spent the rest of the morning sitting on the tailgate of my truck grilling, drinking beer, and venting our frustrations with Checkflight. Chip was still passed out in the back of Rick car, and The Co, who quickly became bored with our conversation, began shotguning beers.

"I'm thinking about quitting aviation altogether." Rick told me. "It's just not turning out to be what I imagined it would be."

Rick shared the same feelings as many pilots these days. When the only job you can get in your field is as bad as Checkflight, suddenly other career paths start to look much brighter.

"Yeah," I agreed with Rick, "aviation's not looking to promising these days, but what are you planning on doing?"

"I don't know; I just think, maybe it's time to start looking at other things. Anything's better than this."

"You know most other jobs require sleeves, especially for the interview. You may have to reattach them."

"I'm not reattaching my sleeves!" Rick was dead serious. "I'll just have to find a job that doesn't require them."

"I just wish I could get a job at a decent airline; too bad none of them are hiring."

"What's so bad about working at Checkflight?" The Co asked. "It's easy. You just ride around in an airplane all day."

"Yeah, you may just ride around all day," I said, "but, we actually have to work. And, all your screw-ups are putting my certificates on the line."

"What certificates?" The Co asked.

"My pilot's certificates; I've worked pretty hard for them, and I don't want to lose them."

"I don't know what you're talking about." The Co said, as he stabbed into another beer can. "You guys complain too much, I'm just happy I've got a job."

A hated to admit it, but The Co did have a point; at least we had a job. "Yeah, I guess you're right." I said, while watching The Co shotgun another beer.

A few of my neighbors gave us dirty looks when they came out to get their Sunday paper. Anytime you're standing in a parking lot with a charcoal grill going, drinking a beer at nine a.m. people always look at you funny.

One of my neighbors stood on his porch, watching for several minutes as The Co puked into a storm drain.

Upon noticing that he was being watched, The Co held out a beer can and yelled to the guy, "Hey man, come down and join the party. You want a beer?"

The man quickly turned around, retreating to the safety of his apartment.

I was pretty sure most of my neighbors thought that we were crazy and I don't think they liked me much. The week prior, when we were blasting music at five AM, someone had pounded on the door. I quickly shut the music and lights off, and checked the peep hole, but I couldn't see anyone.

The Co, who was looking out the window, said, "There's not a cop car outside. Don't answer it."

"Are you sure?" I asked.

"Yeah, it's not the cops. It's probably just a neighbor coming to complain. Neighbors give up and go away. They'll be gone in a minute," The Co said, and then turned the stereo back on.

Two days later, I got a notice of noise violation on my door from the leasing office, but at least it was just a warning; there was no fine. So … whatever.

When I woke up that evening, the sun was already setting. *What day is it?*

I went into the bathroom, to find some Tylenol; my head was pounding. When I looked in the mirror, I saw a tiny spec of glitter on my cheek. Then I remembered the strip club, and made a mental note to check my bank account balance to see if I needed to report my debit card stolen as of yesterday. I picked the spec of glitter off my face and flicked it into the sink.

The Co was lying face down on the living room floor with his shoes still on and a beer in his hand. Chip and Rick must've already gone home.

The Co got up a few minutes later. He saw that he still had the beer in his hand and finished it.

"Isn't that a little warm?" I asked.

He just shrugged his shoulders, and threw the empty can in the trash. "Well, I'm gonna take off," he said.

"I'll see you at work tomorrow," I said, and as he turned away from me, I saw the light shimmer on his face. *Glitter.*

The next day, when I got to work, Chip's car was in the parking lot, still all smashed up. Only now the windshield was shattered too. *Did he wreck again on the way home?*

I found Chip at the weather computer going over wind data. "What happened to your windshield?" I asked.

"I parked under a tree yesterday when I got home," Chip said. "A tree limb fell on it."

"That sucks. Did you ever figure out what you hit the other

night?"

"No, I have no idea. I don't even remember it."

"You smashed it up pretty good."

"Yeah, and it gets worse; Sunday night, when I woke up, I found a whole stack of ATM receipts from the strip club in my pockets."

"How much?"

"Six grand. I must've been giving that girl hundreds at a time. I'm such an idiot."

"No wonder she spent the whole night on your lap."

"What a mistake, I cleaned out my bank account and wrecked my car all in one night."

"Well," I told Chip. "Partying with freight dogs ain't easy."

- 7 -
A Hard Day's Night

It was getting to be winter time, which meant ice, snow, freezing rain, wind, and low approaches. Some days, if you're lucky, you'll get all of those in the same day. This happened to be one of those lucky days. One of the first snow storms of the year was sweeping through the eastern part of the country tonight. The weather looked awful.

The Co and I were flying a route that would take us through Buffalo and then up to Plattsburgh, New York. Pilots have nickname for Buffalo: it's Buffa-snow, and you can guess why. Plattsburgh is in the Adirondack Mountains near the Canadian border, basically the great white north. I think their summer only lasts like two days; they have fall for an afternoon, and then it's winter again.

The snow was coming down hard in Ohio when The Co and I were getting ready to depart. We were sitting in the plane, watching the hangar doors open. Tony, who also worked the line at Checkflight, as well being our only mechanic, was hooking the tow bar up to the nose gear on our Navajo. The other end of the tow bar was attached to the trailer hitch on his Camaro, which also served as our tug.

Our old tug had broken down shortly before The Chief had hired Tony, and the fact that Tony's car had a trailer hitch was what really gave him the upper hand against all the other parolee's The Chief had been interviewing for the open mechanic position. "It's a three for the price of one deal." The Chief had said, "We get a mechanic, a line guy, and a new tug."

With the tow bar now secure, Tony reached under the hood of his car to start it. Blue smoke clouded our windscreen, and filled the hangar, as the Camaro Tug rumbled to life. I couldn't see a thing through the smog, but moments later I felt a jerk, and we began to roll forward.

Once it looked like we were clear of the hangar, I fired the Navajo's engines up. The ramp was a sea of blowing snow and smoke from Tony's car, which was still hooked to the front of the plane. I could barely see our wingtips. In fact, the only thing I could see was the occasional flame that would shoot through the smoke just off our nose accompanied by the rumble of the Camaro Tug's engine, as Tony continually revved it to keep it from dying.

Navajo engines take forever to warm up when it's cold, so while I waited, I listened to the automated weather report for the airport. It was low visibility and low cloud ceilings with heavy snow. "Braking action reports* are in effect," it said at the end of the recorded message.

*- Braking action reports are given when the runway surface is contaminated with snow and ice. After each plane lands, the pilots report on how slick the runway surface was using a scale of good, fair, poor, and nil. Nil means no traction at all. Nil is the report you give as the plane is sliding off the end of the runway.

By the time the engines reached operating temperature, the wings were already covered in a layer of heavy, wet snow, the kind that really sticks to the airplane. I quickly ran the engines up, so we could get the plane back inside to clear off the wings before the work arrived.

The run-up went poorly as usual. The left engine quit when I shut its' right magneto* off, thus confirming that the left engine's left magneto, which had been dead for weeks, was still dead.

*- The magneto's, like the distributor in a car, power the spark plugs. There are two magnetos per engine, so in the event that one should fail in flight, the engine would still run.

Airplanes are built redundantly like this to improve their reliability. At Checkflight, however, any redundant system was considered unnecessary and not worthy of repair.

I shut the right engine down and yelled to Tony to push us back into the hangar.

Back inside, I climbed out of the plane, and made my way through the haze towards the front of the hangar. "Tony! We're you at!" I yelled.

Tony suddenly appeared out of the fog in front of me. "I'm right here."

"Hey, you know that magneto on the left engine is still dead?"

"Yeah?"

"Well are you ever going to fix it?"

"Doubt it."

"Yeah, I didn't think so." *Why do I even bother?*

I grabbed the broom that was sitting in the corner and spent the next ten minutes sweeping the snow off of the wings.

When the work arrived, the courier and I loaded the plane in the hangar, then I had Tony Camaro tug the plane outside again.

As soon as the tow bar was unhooked, I started the engines and called for taxi. We needed to move quickly and get in the air before the snow started to freeze on the wings. If the wings froze up before we got to the runway, we'd have to de-ice, as least that's what the FAA would recommend we do. The Chief, however, would recommend otherwise.

De-ice fluid is expensive, so The Chief tried to deter its use as much as possible. Keeping the plane in a warm hanger until it was time to depart, and then hauling ass to the runway saved money. And The Chief was all about saving money.

When we got to the runway, we were immediately cleared for takeoff. I flipped the wing light on to see if any snow was sticking to the plane yet. There was already a little bit of snow on top of the wings but it wasn't too bad. I lined up on the runway centerline, set takeoff power, and we were off.

Just seconds after becoming airborne, I heard dispatch calling us on our company frequency. "101, this is dispatch," Karen said.

"This is 101, go ahead," I responded.

"We need you to come back. There's a piece of work that got left behind."

"Are you serious? We're already in the air."

"Yeah, it's an important piece. The courier just found it in his trunk. I guess it was stuck under something."

"Alright, but you know we're gonna be late now." Due to the low overcast ceilings tonight and poor visibility, we would have to fly an instrument approach back to the airport. This was going to cause a huge delay.

"Why will you be late?" Karen asked.

This was typical of our dispatchers. They had no idea what it took to fly an airplane in this kind of weather. Karen probably thought turning back to the airport was no more difficult than pulling your car back into the driveway after backing out. "The ceilings are low," I told her. "We're gonna have to shoot an approach to get back in. It's gonna take a few minutes"

"I don't get it, you just left. Why can't you just turn around and come back?"

"It not that simple Karen."

"Well, we need you to come back and get this piece."

"Okay, we're coming back."

"Thanks. I guess, you'll just have to try and make up time once you takeoff again."

I laughed at this. *Make up time, today?* I thought. In this weather we'd be lucky to run on schedule without having to turn around. If we got behind, like we were about to, catching up would be near impossible. "Sure," I said, sarcastically. "We'll try."

I let air traffic control know that we needed to return to the airport. He advised us on what approach to expect and gave us a heading. I flipped the wing light on to check for ice. Even in the short time we'd been airborne, the wings were already loading up and there was a little on the windshield. I cycled the de-ice boots to break some of the ice off of the leading edges of the wings.

"Checkflight 101, fly heading two-seven-zero, maintain three thousand till established, cleared for the ILS two-four." The approach controller said.

I read back our approach clearance. "Checkflight 101, two-seven-zero, three thousand till established, cleared for the ILS two-four."

"Checkflight 101, contact tower one-one-eight-point-five."

"Checkflight 101, calling the tower."

I switched to the tower frequency. "Tower, this is Checkflight

101 on the ILS two-four."

"Weren't you just here?" he asked.

"Yup. A piece of work got left behind."

"Bad day for that. The RVR is eighteen hundred. You're cleared to land runway two-four; braking action is poor."

"Thanks, cleared to land two-four."

At three hundred feet we broke out of the clouds. Snow bombarded the windshield, but the runway gradually came into view. Landing in heavy snow looks kind of like you are moving at hyper speed in the Millennium Falcon. It messes with you a little by affecting your depth perception, making it difficult to judge your height above the runway.

I held a slow rate-of-descent, till … thump. The wheels touched down, I eased on the brakes. Traction was minimal, and the tires glided across the surface of the snow. I pulled the control yoke back, deflecting the elevator upwards, using it as an aerodynamic brake. Gradually our speed decreased, the tires gained some grip, and after using three quarters of the length of the runway, we were finally slowed down.

I made a slow turn onto taxiway charlie and headed for the ramp.

The Co picked his head up; he'd been asleep since we left the ramp the first time. "Are we in Buffalo?" he asked, looking around confused. "How long have I been asleep?"

"About twenty minutes." I said. "We're back at home, a package got left behind."

"Damn!" The Co said, as he slumped back into his reclined seat. "Wake me up when we get to Buffalo, so I can get some dinner."

Though for different reasons, The Co looked just as disappointed as I imagined the banks would be that our arrival in Buffalo would now be behind schedule.

"I don't think there's going to be enough time to get dinner—" I started to say. Then I realized what The Co meant by dinner— the FBO in Buffalo had free popcorn. "Oh, you mean popcorn. Don't worry I'll wake you up."

Upon entering the ramp, I killed the engines and the plane rolled to a stop.

The courier, who had apparently been standing there waiting for us the whole time, was covered in snow. He ran up to the plane with the package in hand.

I popped the side door open. The package was just a small bag that must have weighed only a few ounces. "This must be important," I said, when he handed it to me.

"Sorry," he said, "I thought I had everything, but just after you guys left, I saw that I had a flat tire on my car. When I pulled the spare out of the trunk, I found this bag stuck underneath."

"It happens."

I was about to throw the package over my shoulder into the rear cargo area when the tag on it caught my attention. "ATL," was printed in big bold letters. "Wait, this says Atlanta."

"What? Lemme' see that." The courier said.

I handed the small package back to the courier who examined the routing tag for a moment.

"I don't think that's for us." I told him. "We're not going to Atlanta."

"Shit! This must have been left in my trunk from another delivery." He examined the date that was printed on the tag. "It's from last week."

Great, I thought, all this for a package that's not even for us. However, I wasn't surprised.

Things like this were a regular occurrence around here. Work often went missing and was rarely found. Sometimes, dispatch would pester us for a week to look for the same missing piece of work. "Can you check your aircraft for a missing piece of work?" Karen would ask over and over, even though I'd already told her at least ten times, "it's not in there!"

It was also normal for work to be loaded on the wrong flights. Mis-sorts, they're called, and they were most commonly discovered upon arriving at your destination. That's when you'd realize that you're in Detroit, but the work on board your plane was supposed to go to Cincinnati. In this situation there would most likely be another pilot on the ground in Cincinnati, who's just realizing that all the work on his plane was supposed to go to Detroit.

But, in the last week, I hadn't heard anything about a missing Atlanta piece. "Well, has anyone reported it missing?" I asked the courier.

"No, I don't think so."

"Just throw it out," The Co, who was now taking interest in the conversation, said.

"Huh?" I questioned.

"If no one is missing it, just throw it out." The Co reiterated. At Checkflight we always had the customer's best interest in mind.

"You know that's not a bad idea." The courier said.

I thought about this for a second and came to the conclusion that; any customer, who was still choosing to do business with Checkflight at this point, probably had this coming. "Well, whatever," I said, "we've gotta get going, so do what you want with it."

"Alright, sorry I called you guys back for nothing." The courier apologized. "See ya." He walked away, and pitched the bag of work into the trash can just inside the hangar.

We had a problem now though. The wings were all iced up.

Between the ice we'd collected in the air and the snow that had accumulated since we'd been back on the ground, we either needed to go back in the hangar for a while, or de-ice.

There was no time to put the plane back in the hangar and wait for it to thaw out. We were already way past our departure time. It was a half hour ago when we left here the first time. De-icing was the only option.

I called dispatch on the radio to request de-ice.

"Can't you just put the plane back in the hangar?" Karen asked.

"Sure," I said, "if you don't care that we won't leave for another half hour." What did she think the hangar was some sort of magic ice removing chamber?

"You know, I'll have to get an approval for de-ice from The Chief," she said, "and I doubt he's going to approve it."

"Well, tell him if we can't de-ice, we're not leaving."

I guarantee Checkflight was the only airline in the world where the pilot has to ask for permission to de-ice a plane covered with snow and ice. The Chief saw de-icing as a luxury, not a necessity. He would rather have us take our chances to save a little cash.

A couple minutes later, Karen was back on the radio, "The Chief said you can de-ice, but it's coming out of your paycheck."

"No! Tell him we're not going then, he can find someone else to fly... And, remind him that the longer we have to wait, the later we're going to be."

"I'll tell him, hang on."

A few minutes passed, then, "Okay, he said you can de-ice, but only because we don't have anyone on standby to cover for you; otherwise he said you would have been fired."

"Thanks Karen."

We continued to wait while ten minutes passed, finally, the

hangar door opened. Tony came out with the de-ice truck, which was actually just a two-gallon pump garden sprayer that was filled with god knows what. We still called it "the de-ice truck" though, because it sounded more professional.

Tony pumped the canister, and sprayed down our wings, with what was probably just warm water. Maybe, at best, it may have had a little isopropyl alcohol mixed in. I never knew for sure, as I was always too afraid to ask.

What you don't know can't hurt you, I told myself, during the taxi to the runway, as I watched the "de-ice fluid" freeze into a thin glaze over the wings.

Once airborne— for the second time— and climbing, it didn't take long to start icing up again. At this point, we were running forty-five minutes behind schedule, and I didn't see things getting any better. I don't know how the hell Karen thought we would be making up time.

The ice laden Navajo's performance was weak, and our rate of climb diminished steadily the further we got into the soup. I started to wonder if we'd ever make it to our cruising altitude of nine thousand feet. Air traffic control had informed me that the cloud tops were at eight thousand and it was clear skies above. If we could just make it to eight, we'd be in the clear, although we'd still be carrying all the ice we'd collected in the climb-out, at least we wouldn't be picking up anymore. But, at about seven thousand the plane ran out of steam. The wings were heavy with ice, and the rate-of-climb dropped from positive to neutral, it hung there for a few seconds then dropped negative.

We were going down.

I pitched the nose down, increasing the descent to pick up speed, and blew the boots. The extra speed increased the boots effectiveness, and several large chucks of ice broke free from the wings. I pitched up again, exchanging speed for climb performance. Now slightly lighter on ice, the plane eked its way back into a climb.

Seven thousand five-hundred feet passed we were still slowly climbing.

Seven thousand nine-hundred feet passed. "We're almost there." I announced to The Co who was asleep and could care less even if he were awake.

At Eight thousand feet the altimeter inched higher, but we were still in the clouds. *I hope the controller was right about the tops*, I thought. Then crossing through eight thousand one-hundred feet, the clouds cleared. There was nothing but stars above.

I could relax a little, for now.

The snow in Buffalo was just as bad and as it had been in Ohio, and the wind was worse. "There have been several reports of severe turbulence on the approach." The controller had warned me as he vectored us towards the localizer.

I quickly found that the reports had been dead on, and about the only thing I remember from the approach, which closely resembled a bad roll-over car accident, was at one-point yelling, "Holy shit, if I blink for a second, we're gonna eat the dirt!"

Bursting out of the clouds, knife-edge, just a couple hundred feet from the ground, I rolled the plane upright, spotted the swirling tornado of blowing snow that was the runway, and planted the wheels on it. The plane tried to weather-vane and slide sideways in the strong cross winds. I held the rudder pedal to the floor, opposite the direction of the wind, to keep the nose straight, and rolled the ailerons towards the wind, minimizing our drift. Easing on the brakes we slid across the icy runway, and for the second time tonight, it took a whole lot of room to get stopped.

The courier had been waiting for us for over an hour, and he made sure we knew it.

"Our courier screwed up, we had to turn back, and all this weather is causing us delays. Nothing I can do about it." I told him. As I was saying this, The Co jumped off the wing, and tried to make a fast break for the FBO. "No time for popcorn." I stopped him, "I need you to load the plane while I run inside to order fuel and de-ice for us."

"What? Why can't I order the fuel— and stuff?"

"Do you know how much fuel— and stuff we need?" I asked.

"Ahh … twenty gallons."

"Of fuel? How did you come up with that number?"

"Well, I figure my car holds twelve, and this thing's a little bit bigger."

"Yeah, not even close. You load, while I order."

When I walked into the FBO, I heard someone say, "Hey is that one of Checkflight's Navajos?"

I turned to towards the voice, to see a monkey-suit equipped corporate pilot standing there. "Yes." I answered him.

"I thought so. I used to work at Checkflight back in the day. Is The Chief still running that place?"

"Yup, when did you work there?"

"I left in ninety-eight. Had some great times working there, I miss it sometimes. Is Steve still a captain over there?"

"No. He got let go a couple years ago. Checkflight's not what it used to be; trust me, you're not missing anything."

"Oh … sorry to hear that."

"Hey who are you flying for now?"

"A charter op out of Richmond, it's a pretty good gig."

"You guys hiring?"

"No sorry man, we've got a couple guys on furlough. Its rough times ya know."

"Oh yeah, I know, but hey it was worth a shot right."

"Always, hey, fly safe in that old Navajo."

"Will do, see ya around."

With the work loaded, our fueling done, and de-ice on the way, I made sure all the cargo compartments were closed properly. I didn't want to make that mistake again, especially not tonight. *Even worse*, I thought, would be having a cabin door open up in flight. In this weather it'd get awful cold real quick, so I double checked the latch after getting in.

Before getting de-iced, I called clearance delivery to make sure there wouldn't be any delays for our departure. Once you've been de-iced, you're on a time limit to get in the air.

De-ice fluid only works for so long; if we got to the runway and there was a delay, it would all be a waste.

The controller told me that there were no delays, so I gave the go ahead for the de-ice truck to spray us down. It was a welcome change of pace to have a real de-ice truck spraying us down with real de-ice fluid. The Chief would not be happy about this, but by the time he got the bill for it, it would be far too late to return the fluid.

Once they were done spraying us, I called ground control for taxi. "Checkflight 101, expect a thirty-minute delay for east-bound departures," he told me.

"What? I just asked clearance if there would be any delays, and he told me no."

"Sorry, the delay just went into effect."

"Ridiculous!"

I picked up the hand mic, and for a second, contemplated keying it up and banging it on the instrument panel, just to make sure the controller knew how pissed I was. *Nah*, I thought, it's not going to help anything.

"Might as well shut it down," I said, as I pulled the fuel into cut-off. "Looks like we're going to be waiting for a while."

The Co was happy about the news. "Sweet, I'm gonna go get some popcorn inside," he said, springing from his seat.

"Alright, but come right back, because if they call us, I want to get out of here quick." I felt like the parent of a small child when I said this, and I even found it necessary to add; "I'm serious!"

"Alright, alright, don't worry, I'll hurry." The Co said, as he jumped over the cargo net, climbing over bags and boxes, trying to make his way towards the rear cabin door.

A rush of cold wind filled the cabin. The Co wiggled his way through the bottom half of the rear clam-shell. "And, shut that door behind you, it's cold!" I felt the need to remind him.

"Got it." He slammed the door, and ran off across the ramp, disappearing into the blowing snow.

I stayed in the plane monitoring the radios, waiting for our turn to go. A half hour of watching snow pile on our wings went by, and The Co still hadn't come back.

Ground called up. "Checkflight 101, fire em' up and give me a call when you're ready to taxi."

"Checkflight 101. I'll let you know when I'm ready," I responded. Thinking, *where the hell was The Co?*

I called the de-ice truck back to spray us down again, hoping The Co would come walking up any minute now. They showed up pretty quick, but The Co was still nowhere in sight. I jumped out of the plane and ran up to the de-ice truck. "Hang on a second," I said, "I've gotta run inside real quick and get my co-pilot."

"Alright man," he said, "but we can't wait too long; there's a lot of other planes waiting for us."

"I'll be quick," I assured him.

When I got inside the FBO, I ran from room to room looking for The Co. He wasn't around the popcorn machine or the vending area. He wasn't in the bathroom or the flight planning room. I found him in the pilots' lounge, kicked back in a recliner, watching a movie.

"What the hell are you doing?!" I yelled, "we've gotta go!"

The Co nonchalantly turned his head towards me. "I just came in here to relax for a minute, I saw that this movie was on, so I've been watching it. Have you seen it? It's pretty good."

"No, I haven't seen it. We've gotta go, come on."

"Hang on a minute," he pointed towards the TV, "watch this part: it's hilarious."

I grabbed his arm, pulling him up from his seat. "No, I'm serious; we gotta go!"

"Fine," he grumbled, and got up to follow me.

By the time we got back to the plane, the de-ice truck was gone. I called him again, and he said it would be five minutes till he could come back. Then I called ground control up and told him we were still waiting for de-ice.

"Alright," the controller said, "but I've only got a fifteen-minute window to release you. After that, you'll be delayed for another hour."

We sat there for another ten minutes waiting for de-ice to come back. I called him again. "About five minutes," he said. "I'm just finishing up on another plane."

Just then my cell phone rang; it was The Chief. "Hello?"

"Did you just de-ice in Buffalo?" He asked.

"Yes. How did you know?"

"The payment authorization just came through. I don't

remember approving this."

I tried to defend myself. "Approval or not it had to be done."

"Well it's coming out of your paycheck. Where are you now?"

"We're still in Buffalo," I explained the situation, and told him that, due to the delay, we were now waiting for a second de-ice.

"Not approved." The Chief said, "You need go now. You need to get to Plattsburgh immediately."

"But—"

He cut me off. "Listen! If you miss that departure window you're fired, so I suggest you forget about your little de-ice, and leave now!"

"Screw it, we're leaving, bye."

I spun the engines and called for taxi.

We got to the runway just in time to make our departure window, and we were cleared for an immediate takeoff. The plane had snow piled up on the wings, making me a little nervous, but I taxied the plane on the runway and went for it anyway.

"Hope all this snow blows off," I said.

"Why's that?" The Co asked.

I gave The Co a concerned look, "is that a serious question?"

"No."

I gunned the throttles.

During the takeoff roll, the loose snow on top did blow off, but it still wasn't good. There was a three-quarter inch thick layer of rough frozen snow and ice still sticking to every surface of the plane.

A few thousand feet of runway disappeared behind us. The runway edge lights quickly turned from white to amber, indicating that we were running out of room.

Trying to lift off, at too slow an airspeed, with all this snow on the wings, could be disastrous. I thought, we may have to abort. "Come on speed."

Right about the time the runway's centerline lights turned red, indicating only one-thousand feet of runway left, the airspeed finally reached rotation speed; I pulled back on the yoke and put the gear up.

We had used the entire runway to get airborne, clearing the fence at the far end by a mire twenty-five feet. The approach lights for the opposite runway passed just under our wings, and the plane was only climbing two-hundred feet-per-minute at best.

In the soup now, I couldn't see a thing. "Checkflight 101, low altitude alert." The tower warned me. I could hear his warning horn going off in the background while he transmitted.

Low altitude is a warning you never want to hear while in zero visibility, struggling to climb.

"We're climbing." I said. *Or trying to*, I thought, and pushed the throttles as far into the forward stops as they would go.

Several nerve-racking minutes and several low altitude alerts later; the plane had slowly limped its way to a safe altitude.

Following this incident, I decided that I needed to quit caring about The Chief's threats before something bad happened, and I vowed to never take-off with snow frozen to the top of the wings again. *Who cares how late we are,* I thought. We'd probably end up losing this bank's business anyway, so what's the point in rushing.

Our customers hadn't been very happy with our service lately, and I didn't blame them one bit. After the debacle in Cleveland, two banks canceled their contracts with us. They gave the contracts to one of our competitors, a larger company, who they said acted in a much more professional manner. I think we can all thank The Co for that.

At this point, we only had a handful of customers left, and no matter what I did, everyone else around here was bound to piss those last few off. *Let Checkflight's chips fall where they may*, I thought. I needed to shift my focus to covering my own ass.

The next stop was Plattsburgh, New York. I'd only been there once before; it was not a good experience, and I wasn't expecting this time around to be any better.

We would be landing at Plattsburgh Clinton County Airport, a small Podunk field located to the west of the city, in the middle of nowhere. As this airport gets little to no traffic at night, especially in the winter, the control tower and all other airport services would be closed upon our arrival.

There is a large airport, Plattsburgh International, located much closer to the city, which does have twenty-four-hour services available, but they charge a landing fee. We were using the secondary, Clinton County Airport, because it was free. But free came with a price; there would be no fuel, no de-ice, no building to go inside to stay warm, and no fire rescue services if something should go wrong. The last time I was there, I had heard wolves howling in the distance while I waited on the ramp for the courier to arrive. I had decided to wait in the plane.

Due to the terrain, radar services in this area were limited. The approach into Clinton County would require us to self-navigate through the Adirondack Mountains, in the middle of the night, during a snow storm. Not my idea of a good time.

Making our way through upstate New York, we were in radio and radar contact with, Boston Air Traffic Control Center, who controlled this airspace at night.

When we were about sixty miles south of Plattsburgh, the center gave us a waypoint to fly to, at which point we would start the approach into Clinton County. "Checkflight 101, fly direct PUDGY*," the controller instructed us. "Cleared for the ILS one into Clinton County."

*- Waypoints are given five letter pronounceable names, often having some relation to their locale to make them easier to remember, such as; ELVIS in Memphis, SMOGY in Los Angeles, PECHY in Atlanta, and JIMEY BUFIT FINNS PYRUT UTLEY, which is a sequence of waypoints leading into West Palm Beach. As for what PUDGY meant; your guess is as good as mine.

I promptly read back our approach clearance, then, as I was not familiar with the waypoint he had given us, pulled out my charts to look up PUDGY. When I found it on the chart, I realized that due to the limited navigation equipment this antique had, we didn't have the capabilities to fly directly to PUDGY as instructed. The controller had assumed that we would have the modern equipment that everyone else had, but we were thirty years behind the tech curve here.

I weighed my options for a minute. There was another way to get there; by using a waypoint that I could properly identify, but it would take us out of the way. Seeing as that would further add to our late arrival, I decided to just estimate a heading to take us to PUDGY. *That will get us close enough*, I thought, and I made the left turn to the approximated heading.

Moments later I regretted this decision.

No less than an hour ago, I had been telling myself not to do these kinds of things anymore. Like a drug addict trying get sober, I guess the poor decision making The Chief had instilled in me would be a tough habit to kick. There was bound to be a few relapses. *One last time*, I told myself.

The center controller cut in to give us some good news; "Checkflight 101, the last plane to land in Plattsburgh was at ten p.m. (it was now one a.m.); he reported the braking action on the runway as poor with snow. He also said that areas of the taxiway and ramp had nil braking action due to ice patches. That's the latest surface report I have."

"Thanks," I said.

"Checkflight 101, radar service is terminated, you can switch to the advisory frequency*. Contact flight service* to close your flight plan on the ground."

*- An Advisory Frequency is used at airports that do not have an operating control tower. Aircraft using uncontrolled airports can use this frequency to speak to each other, and provide self-traffic control, by way of reporting their position to other aircraft in the vicinity.

An advisory frequency's effectiveness is limited by the quality of the position reports given by each pilot operating near that airport. Many aircraft that operate near uncontrolled airports simply aren't listening to the reports being given, and many that are listening, are very unsure of their own position, making their reports useless.

*- Flight Service is a group of long-winded old men who sit in dark cubicles, droning on and on about insignificant weather conditions and other shit that no one cares about. They are, however, useful for the filing and closing flight plans, and initiating search and rescue operations in the case that an aircraft "doesn't make the airport."

"Checkflight 101, switching to advisory; I'll close my flight plan with flight service on the ground," I responded. "See ya on the way out."

Now forty miles outside Plattsburgh, from this point on, we

would be on our own. In a few minutes, we'd descend below the mountain peaks and our radar blip, on Boston Centers screen, would disappear.

I switched over to Clinton Counties advisory frequency, gave a position report, and asked if any other aircraft were in the area. No one answered.

Since no one was listening I decided not to bother with giving any further reports. I did, however, monitor the frequency for the rest of the way in, on the off chance that someone else was crazy enough to be flying into this airport tonight.

It was a strange lonely feeling navigating down into the mountains on a dark cloudy night with no one tracking your flight or listening to your radio calls. I did have The Co sitting next to me, who was immersed in a video game, but since he wouldn't be contributing to the flight, I might as well have been alone.

We did still have our flight plan open though, which was the only way anyone knew we were even in the air anymore. If we didn't call flight service to close our flight plan within thirty minutes of the time that we should have landed, search and rescue would come looking for us. But that meant if we went down on this approach right now, it would be a least forty minutes until anyone missed us, and probably a whole lot longer till anyone found us.

Ice piled on the wings as I navigated our way onto the approach, and our speed decreased steadily. We passed PUDGY, which I managed to get us pretty close to, and I made the turn to intercept the localizer. Now in a valley, with mountains surrounding us, we had to perform a steep circling descent to get down to the altitude where we would pick up the glideslope, which would lead us down to the runway. I pitched the nose over and banked hard to the right, descending as quickly as possible so we could lose a few thousand feet in one three-hundred- and sixty-degree turn. Rolling out of the turn I picked up the localizer again.

The glideslope slowly came in, and we were now descending towards the runway. I glanced out the side window at the giant horns of ice that were forming on the wingtips. I continued to blow the de-ice boots regularly, but our airspeed loss got worse and worse. It was taking a lot of power to maintain airspeed, and I didn't have much to spare.

While I was focused on flying the instrument approach, The Co was focused on playing his Game Boy.

I asked a stupid question. "Are you paying attention?"

"No," The Co responded, "and your questions are distracting me."

We drifted slightly left course, and I quickly corrected. My eyes were glued to the instruments; this was not the place to make a mistake. "I'm serious, I need your help." I said. "I think we've only got one shot to make this; we've got way too much ice on the plane to go around and try again."

The Co remained focused on his game. "No! I'm at the boss of this level." He declared.

I swatted his hand. "Well, I'm at the boss of this level! And I could use your help right now!"

"God damn it … Fine!" The Co slammed his Game Boy down. "You killed Mario; now what do you want me to do?"

"Keep your head up, tell me if you see the runway."

"I don't see it."

"Well keep looking; we're at three-hundred feet."

"Alright."

"Two-hundred feet; decision height." I announced. This is the point where if you can't see the runway, you must bail-out, and start climbing away from the ground. But, convinced that climbing was no longer an option I pressed on towards the runway.

Decision height came and went with no runway in sight.

"One-hundred feet. Anything?"

"I see lights," The Co said, as the windshield filled with the flash of bright strobe lights that were located at the beginning of the runway.

Moments later, "there's the runway." The Co said in a monotone that greatly undermined the urgency of the situation.

I looked up to see that the runway was completely covered in snow. No asphalt was visible at all; it was a clean white sheet without a single tire track. The only way to tell that a runaway was even there at all was by the white lights sticking out of the snow, lining the runway edges.

We touched down, and the props churned snow up all around us, obstructing my view. The plane lightly swerved from side to side as we slowed.

"The braking action wasn't that bad," I said, as I began making a right turn off the runway … but I spoke to soon. The snow had blown from the corner of the taxiway, right at the edge of the runway leaving a bare spot.

Unknowingly, I made the turn onto the taxiway right on that bare corner. It was pure ice.

"NIL!" I yelled, as the tires instantly lost what little grip they'd had, spinning us and sending us plowing through the taxiway lights, off into the grass, which at the time happened to be under-siege by a couple feet of snow.

I quickly killed the engines as the plane violently spun and bounced through several snow drifts before finally coming to a rest about fifty feet from the nearest pavement.

I looked over at The Co. "You alright?"

"I'm good."

"Shit! What are we gonna do? We're probably stuck!"

"It's cool. Just call for a tug."

"There is no tug. There's no one else here but us."

The Co looked around, as if expecting to see a tug come driving up. "That sucks," he said, "I'm sure a tug will show up though."

"There's no tug! Trust me."

I assessed the situation for a minute, and noticed that the parking lot near the ramp was empty. *Figures, we're late, but the courier's still not here.* Then it hit me. "No one saw us. If we can dig our way out, maybe no one will ever have to know about this." There appeared to be areas between us and the taxiway that weren't that deep. "Call flight service and tell them we landed and don't say anything about being stuck. I'm gonna get out and see how it looks."

The Co looked puzzled. "Who do I call?"

"Flight service."

"What's the number?"

"You don't know the number?"

"No, you always do that stuff."

"Here give me your phone," I said, holding my hand out.

The Co handed me his phone. I dialed the number and gave it back to him. "Just tell them; 'this is Checkflight 101, we landed in Plattsburgh, and we'd like to close our flight plan.' And don't say anything about running off the taxiway or being stuck till we figure this out."

"Gotcha."

While The Co called, I got out to inspect the landing gear. If it was damaged, we might have a big problem. I really did not want to have to call The Chief and explain to him that his plane was stuck in a snow drift. Even though, had we flown into the international airport, where the runways were plowed, this would have never happened. But The Chief would never understand that logic.

Upon inspection, everything looked to be in one piece, but the plane was wedged into a snow drift. It definitely looked like we were stuck; I figured it was worth a shot to try digging though.

I got back in the plane just as The Co was getting off the phone.

"We need to start digging," I said. "I don't see the courier over there; the parking lot looks empty. Call dispatch and ask them how far out he is. He should have been here a long time ago and don't tell them anything about being stuck either." I grabbed my gloves and pulled my hood over my head, cinching the drawstrings tight. "I'm gonna start digging. After you call, come help me."

I jumped back out and started clearing snow away from the wheels like a mad man. Time was of the essence, if the courier showed up, and saw what was going on, it would be hard to keep this a secret.

A couple minutes later The Co climbed out of the plane. "Karen said she's trying to call the courier. She said she'll call us back when she tracks him down."

"Alright, help me dig. If we can get out of here before the courier shows up, no one will ever have to know about it."

Twenty minutes later, my hands were numb, but we had the snow cleared away from the wheels enough that we might be able to power out of it.

We got back in the plane, and I started up the engines. The props churned the loose snow up all around us making it difficult to see. I pulled back on the control yoke to keep weight off the nose wheel and ran the power up. The plane shuddered as I added more and more power; slowly we started to move. We hopped and bounced, putting the landing gear through stress it was probably never engineered to endure, and it took nearly full power to plow though some of the drifts, but eventually we bahaed our way back up onto the taxiway.

I taxied as carefully as possible to the ramp, not wanting to run off into the grass again.

The ramp was small and we would have to make a tight one-eighty to turn around so we could get back out of here. There was a hangar on one side and a fence on the other with snow piled up in the corners. If the ramp were dry, it would be an easy turn to make, but on this ice, it was going to be tough.

I stopped the plane, but kept the engines running. "Get out and marshal me," I said to The Co.

"What do want me to do?"

"Just watch the wing tips while I turn around, and make sure I don't hit anything."

The Co climbed out the back door, and walked around the front of the plane.

I cut the nose wheel to the right, and slowly maneuvered through the turn. The Co stayed in front of the plane as I turned, waving his arms for me to keep going. But, about three-quarters of the way around I stopped. The left wing looked like it was just inches from the side of the building, but from inside I couldn't tell exactly how close.

I pointed to the left-wing tip. The Co looked at it and gave me a thumbs up, so I continued creeping forward.

Then I heard something break.

You've gotta be kidding me, I thought. I shut the engines down and got out to look.

The red nav light on the left wing was smashed against the building. "I thought you said it was clear," I demanded.

"No," The Co said. "I gave you a thumbs up 'cause you were going to hit it."

"Why would you give me a thumbs up if I was going to hit it?"

"'Cause that's what I thought you were asking. 'Am I going to hit it?' So, I gave a thumbs up, meaning 'yes, you're going to hit it.'"

"Thumbs up means good; thumbs up means all clear! It doesn't mean you're going to hit the building!"

"Oh," The Co looked confused. "Well, sorry, I thought you could see that it was going to hit."

"No, I couldn't see! That's the whole reason I had you marshal me! If I could see it, I wouldn't need to be marshaled."

The Co nodded. "Ahh … got'cha, I just thought you wanted me to watch 'cause you were trying to impress me with your turning skills or something."

I shook my head in disbelief. "Come on, we've gotta push this thing back a little so I can pull it forward."

Once the plane was parked in a reasonable spot, I called dispatch again to find out where the courier was. Karen had said she'd call us back and she never did, and it had been awhile.

"Dispatch, this is Karen."

"Hey Karen it's 101; have you heard from that courier yet?"

"What? Where have you guys been? Someone named Flight Service just called here; they said you never closed your— flight plan?"

"We closed our flight plan. The Co called to close it. And he called you too."

"They told me you didn't."

"What?"

"Yeah, they said they were about to start search and rescue, because no one's heard from you, and they asked me if I could get a hold of you, so I tried calling your phone, but there was no answer."

"Well my phone was in the plane when we.... Never mind," I almost blew it. "But didn't The Co call you?"

"No, I haven't heard from him."

"But I saw him on the phone ... hang on..."

I turned to The Co. "You closed our flight plan, didn't you?"

"Ahh ... not really. Bad cell service; the call got dropped."

I couldn't believe this. "Why didn't you tell me?"

"I figured it really didn't matter."

"Didn't matter? They were about to send search and rescue! And what happened when you called dispatch?"

"Same. I'm getting pretty weak service out here."

"But you told me you talked to Karen, and she would call us back? I saw you on the phone."

"Yeah I was just pretending to be on the phone, I figured she'd eventually call us anyway, and if I told you that I didn't get through you would have told me to keep trying." He shrugged his shoulders. "I just didn't feel like it."

"You're freakin' unbelievable," I said. "Hey, Karen, The Co was supposed to close our flight plan and call you; he never did."

"Alright, well, that flight service guy left me his number. I'll let him know we got a hold of you."

"Thanks. And what about the courier? He should have been here a long time ago."

"I'll try to get a hold of him and see where he's at. Just keep waiting. If he's not there in fifteen minutes, call me back."

"We'll be here," I said, and hung up.

When I got off the phone, I turned to The Co. "You suck." I said.

"You suck." He responded.

"Alright ... well, let's get all this ice off the plane."

The Co looked around, as if trying to find an escape route. "Okay, but I'm gonna go take a leak first," he said.

"Fine, but hurry up, 'cause we need to get all this crap off the plane so we're ready to go when the courier shows up."

"Yeah, yeah, whatever." The Co said, as he disappeared around the side of the hangar building.

The good news was; it had quit snowing shortly after we landed, which meant, for the first time tonight we wouldn't have to worry about the plane icing up while it sat here on the ground. But there was still the matter of removing all of the ice we had collected in the air on the way in here, which was frozen in thick chunks to every forward-facing surface of the plane.

I got my flashlight out of my flight bag and started using the back of it to chip ice off the wings. There was no de-ice truck here to spray us down, and no warm hangar to put the plane in. Pounding the crap out of wings with the back of a flashlight was the best we had.

I made my way around the plane, cracking and then breaking off the huge horns that stuck out from wingtips, the thick slabs that covered the front of the engine cowlings, the cones frozen to the prop spinners, and every other chunk that was stuck to the wings, tail, landing gear, antennas, vents, air intakes, probes, and every other protrusion. It was a primitive, labor intensive, means of removing ice, but it worked. Twenty minutes later, the plane was clean, piles ice chunks littered the ramp, but The Co still hadn't come back.

"Co!" I yelled. No answer.

I walked around the side of the hangar building, in the direction that he had gone. As soon as I turned the corner, there he was. He had been hiding back there the whole time, probably so he wouldn't have to help chip ice.

"Have you just been standing back here?"

"Ahh, maybe."

"You know I could've used your help."

"Yeah, about that, you're like a slave driver; this is just too much work for me. I already helped you find the runway when we were landing, and you still haven't apologized for messing up my game; it took me a long time to get to that level. And then I helped you with the digging; it's just enough for one day. I needed a break."

I saw red. I felt like sewing The Co's ass to his face.

For a moment I glared in his eyes, trying to find the words to express my anger. Suddenly, I lunged at him and grabbed his shoulders while I swung my left leg under him, sweeping him off his feet. The Co crashed down face first into a snow pile, and I pinned him down with my foot on his back. I grabbed his hair and repeatedly pushed on the back of his head, shoving his face into the cold snow. "What the hell man!" He yelled.

"Sorry I screwed up your game, dick!"

Then, figuring he'd had enough I let go of his hair and removed my foot from his back. But, as soon as I did, he rolled over, grabbed my arm and pulled me down.

The Co quickly scrambled, rolling over on top of me, he pinned me down and began taking handfuls of snow and shoving them down the back of my shirt. "Slave driver!" He screamed.

I kicked up, and he fell to the side.

"Yeah, well, you're the worst co-pilot I've ever had!" I said as we both jumped to our feet.

We stood there for a minute, facing each other in a wrestling stance, staring into the others eyes, both of us shifting from side to side, waiting for the other to make a move.

I was out of breath. It was freezing cold out, my hands were numb, and my back was now soaked. The Co's face was bright red.

He sniffled and wiped his nose. "Come on man, truce," I said. "Let's go sit in the plane and get some heat."

I stuck out my hand.

The Co looked at me with skepticism for a moment before finally letting his guard down. "Truce," he said, and shook my hand.

We both brushed ourselves off, and I shook the snow out of the back of my shirt.

When we climbed in the plane, I started up one of the engines to power the heater, and I called dispatch again to see if there had been any word on the courier.

"I can't get a hold of him," Karen said, "just keep waiting."

"We'll be here," I said again, and hung up.

I rubbed my hands together and stuck them right in front of the heat vent. The Co and I were both soaked and shivering. "It freakin' cold out here," The Co said. "I hope that heater keeps up." Navajo heaters are prone to failure, especially when you really need them. I'd be just our luck if this thing quit right now.

"I hope so," I said. "I've got it on high."

Several minutes passed as The Co and I sat in awkward silence.

"Did I ever tell you about the first time I flew with Chip?" I asked, breaking the silence.

"No," The Co said. I was sure he could care less about my story, but I had nothing else to do, so he was gonna have to listen to it.

"Well, you're not the first co-pilot I pushed down in the snow," I began.

"Last winter Chip and I were at Chicago Midway during a horrible blizzard. We had been there for several hours, and the plane had been sitting outside in the snow. About a half-hour before our departure time, I sent Chip out to warm the engines up, and while he was doing that, I swept the snow off the wings with a broom.

Once the engines were warm, we loaded the work. But the whole time, Chip kept asking me, 'Are you sure you want to go?'

I had heard that he was afraid of flying, especially flying in bad weather, so I was expecting some resistance from him, and the weather was pretty bad that night. I just kept telling him to relax though. 'We'll be fine,' I told him over and over.

When it was time to go, I jumped in the plane to get the taxi clearance, and I told him to wipe the windshield off real quick then get in.

But he still kept asking, 'Are we really going?'

I told him, 'Yes,' and gave him one of my gloves to clear off the windshield.

He just stood there whining, saying 'I don't think we should go.'

I said. 'We're going! Just wipe off the windshield so I can see the taxiway.'

He finally did it and we took off.

During the climb-out, we got rocked pretty good until we reached about four thousand feet or so, then it started to smooth out. And, that's when I started to notice that it was freakin' cold in the plane. I thought, shit, I'd been so focused on dealing with the horrible weather during the takeoff and climb-out that I forgot to turn the heater on. But I looked down, and the heater switch was on. So, I messed with it for a few minutes, but there was still no heat.

I gave up; It definitely wasn't working.

We were flying to St. Louis which would be an hour and fifteen-minute flight, and it was *cold*. The outside air temperature gauge was showing negative twenty-two Celsius. I bundled up as much as I could and put my gloves on. Of course, one of them was covered in snow from wiping the windshield off, but I put it on anyway because it was all I had.

By the time we got to St. Louis, I was so cold I could barely move. My fingers were frozen stiff, and I still had snow on my shoes from Chicago.

And, that's when Chip told me that he had over-temped the heater when he was warming the engines up in Chicago. He said, he forgot to run the blower so it overheated and the fuse blew, and that he knew the heater was broke before we left Chicago. But, because he was afraid that I would be mad, he didn't say anything; instead, he just tried to talk me out of going.

I was so pissed that I shoved him, and he slipped and fell on the icy ramp."

When I finished my story, I looked over at The Co. He was fast asleep. I knew he wouldn't listen but . . . oh well.

For the next couple hours, I just sat there, waiting, bored out of my mind.

Since I had to keep an engine running to power the heater, after a while, I started to worry that if the courier didn't show up soon, we wouldn't have enough fuel left to get back to Ohio. There was no fuel here, which meant we might have to make an extra fuel stop on the way home. But, just then, at about five in the morning, I spotted headlights down the road. I nudged The Co awake. "The courier's here," I said.

The car pulled up in the parking lot near the fence.

"Start unloading," I told The Co.

I got out and walked up to the fence. "What happened?" I asked. "Where have you been?"

"Well, I wrecked my car into a snow bank," the Canadian courier said, as he pointed to his busted-up bumper. "I had to dig myself out. It took forever, and I left my headlights on while I was digging so I could see what I was doing. By the time I dug the car out, the battery was dead, and the car wouldn't start. So, I had to call someone to come give me a jumpstart."

"Well, I guess everyone is having a bad night tonight."

The courier started pulling bags and boxes out of his trunk and throwing them over the barbwire fence to me. The gate in the fence was locked at night, so the only thing we could do was throw the stuff over.

The Co dragged over the work that we had for the courier, and we started throwing our stuff over to his side, until I came to the last box, it was marked "Extremely Fragile."

"You think I should throw this?" I asked. I held the box up so the courier could see it.

"Go for it, I'll catch it," the courier said.

"Alright, here it goes." I threw the box like I was shooting a free throw over the fence towards the courier. He caught it.

"Nice catch. First thing that went right all night."

The courier left, and The Co and I loaded up our stuff and got back in the plane. I thought about calling dispatch to let them know that the courier had finally arrived. Then I thought, *nah, let her wonder*, remembering the fact that after several hours of waiting here, Karen had never called us back.

I had to call flight service and file a new flight plan since our old one had long since expired. I picked up our departure clearance from them as well.

It was a long slow taxi to the runway on the icy taxiways. When we got there, I lined up on the sheet of snow, halfway in between the white lights on each side of us, and firewalled it.

A cloud of snow kicked up all around us as we fishtailed down the slick runway into the darkness.

Alex Stone

Driving home that morning, I thought about how horrible the night had been. I turned on my radio and heard The Beatles singing "A Hard Day's Night." For a minute, I sang along. Then it hit me: John Lennon never flew through ice; Paul McCartney never encountered severe turbulence. Maybe George shoved snow down the back of Ringo's shirt once or twice ... still, "The Beatles don't know what a hard day's night is," I said to myself. But I turned the radio louder and continued singing anyway.

Part Two:
We Will Now Begin Our Descent

- 8 -
Drumming Up Some Business

Business had been slow at Checkflight lately. The declining economy and rising fuel prices had made things difficult for the aviation industry. In addition to that, the waning use of the paper check, and the implementation of electronic check transfer had especially hurt us. Electronic check transfer meant that many of our customers no longer had a need for shipping physical checks, which had been the core of our business for years. But, by far, our biggest problem was that our customers were losing faith in us. We were always late, breaking down, or losing our cargo over a major metropolitan area.

The Chief had always been on the shady side of things. He built this place by getting by on the bare minimum. But lately, in his attempts to stay profitable, he had been resorting to business practices that were even more questionable than usual.

Recently, he had announced that the company would no longer be providing hotels on overnight stays. He told us that we could sleep in the back of the airplane, in the airport lounge, or, if requested, we may be provided with a company-issued tent which must be returned at the end of the trip. "I feel by cutting out unnecessary hotel expenses," he'd said, "we will ensure our company's profitability into the future."

All of the pilots took large pay cuts as well. I was now making less than I did when I started working here four years ago, which has left me wondering why I was still working here when I could be making more as a factory worker or maybe even a trash collector.

Then came the incident in which Rick caught The Chief pouring regular automotive gasoline into one of the airplane's fuel tanks with an ordinary gas can. When Rick asked him what was going on, The Chief said he was just "mixing in a little."

"It's a lot cheaper than Avgas," The Chief defended. "It won't hurt anything, and it will help reduce our fuel costs."

"You could have at least used premium," Rick suggested.

Later that evening, the same airplane that Rick had witnessed The Chief filling with auto gas had a dual flame-out in flight. Both engines quit as a result of the low-grade gasoline, leaving the pilots with a rapidly descending Navajo glider. Without an airport in gliding range, luckily the pilots were able to safely dead-stick the plane onto a highway near Pittsburgh, and for a moment it appeared that they and the plane would immerge from the incident unscathed. But, seconds after touching down on the busy expressway, as the captain tried to merge through traffic towards the shoulder, the plane was intentionally rear ended by a road raged commuter, who later claimed he did it because; "they were taking up the whole damn carpool lane!"

While The Chief wasted his time coming up with these money saving schemes, most of which hurt us more than they helped, our competitors had been looking for new types of cargo to fly to replace checks and carry their airlines into the future. Up till recently The Chief had held his stance that; debit cards and electronic check transfer were just a fad, "Checks will come back around," he'd always told us. But lately his tone had changed. It seemed that even The Chief was now starting to realize that paper checks were a thing of the past, and he was now trying to drum up new business opportunities, though I was none too pleased with what he was coming up with. In fact, it seemed as though The Chief was after the most inappropriate cargo he could find.

We were now flying live farm animals that treated the back of the airplanes like a stable, which I quickly found to be a little distracting. I mean these animals were just loose in the plane, and trying to fly while a goat is chewing on the back of your seat or having rooster crows interrupt your radio calls did not make the safest cockpit environment. And no one was going to clean up the mess that these animals were leaving behind. If we (the pilots) didn't do it, it wouldn't get done. After all, we're the only ones that have to spend time in these airplanes, and flying a plane that smells like a barn gets old real quick.

The Chief had also attempted to have us fly passengers in the back of our cargo planes. When we asked him how this would work, seeing as how there are no seats back there, he responded, "People don't need a seat; the regulations only state that a passenger must have a seat belt. So, give them a piece of rope, have them tie it to the cargo tie downs, and it'll be perfectly legal."

Of course, this information was not to be disclosed to the poor unsuspecting customers who actually bought tickets for our new commuter service, "that is," The Chief had told us, "until they arrive at the airport, at which point their tickets are non-refundable."

Most stormed off in anger either upon learning this, or seeing the sad state of their potential chariot. However, some, out of the desperate need to get to their destination, reluctantly chose to ride, often leaving worse a mess in the back of the airplanes than the farm animals.

Our commuter airline was short lived though, as it drew the attention of the FAA, who promptly revised the regulations to state that "a passenger must have a seat belt *and a seat*," putting us quickly out of the passenger flying business.

But just when I thought that The Chief's hare-brained schemes had hit a new low, he found a way to go lower.

The Chief called me into his office one day to inform me he had a flight for The Co and me to do.

"It's a little different than your normal thing," he said.

"How so?"

"Well, you're going to be flying cargo between two farms, sort of."

"More animals?"

"No, it's not animals, it's crops, and you will be picking them up directly on the farm." The Chief leaned back in his chair and put his feet up on his folding table.

"Why do we have to pick them up on the farm?" I asked. "Why can't they deliver them to the airport like everything else?"

I could tell he was beating around the bush here, but I wasn't quite sure where he was going with this.

"Well," he said, "these are the kind of crops you can't bring to the airport. The customer would prefer it if we pick them up directly from their farm, and then deliver directly to their people on another farm, in another state."

"It's a drug run, isn't it?"

"Well, sort of," he responded, "but it's cargo just like anything else we fly. The only difference is that the pickup and drop off locations are a little more remote."

"Are you kidding me? It's not like everything else—it's drug trafficking! Is this what we are resorting to, being common criminals?"

He sat up again, obviously upset with my accusations. "It's not like we're crossing international borders," The Chief defended. "It's all within the country, and, besides, we need the business. And they pay well."

"It's still moving illegal substances across state lines; and I could care less what they pay."

"Well if crossing state lines is your issue, would you do it if the flight was within one state?" He asked, "because, if this goes well, they may have a lot more flights for us, and some of those may be within one state."

"No! I'm not doing it at all. I put way too much on the line for this company, and this is just going too far."

"You know there are a lot of unemployed pilots out there that would love to have your job." The Chief reminded me.

He had me. But I could top him. "If you fire me over this, I'll turn you over to the Feds in a second."

"Relax, I'm not going to fire you, but I am going to find someone else to fly this run."

"That's fine." I said, "find someone else to fly it. I want nothing to do with this!"

And he did.

It took The Chief all of five minutes to find someone else. I should have known that The Co would jump all over this opportunity like it was the greatest thing to ever happen to him. He actually said, "This is the greatest thing to ever happen to me!"

He was even willing to donate his pay to any captain that would fly the drug run with him. "As long as I get a little tip from the customer on the side?" he requested.

"I think that can be arranged," The Chief replied.

The Co and The Chief were quite pleased with their little arrangement, but I wasn't. Ultimately, this incident would bring us from the level of being a slightly shady airline to that of a downright illegal one. I had been fine with flying busted-up airplanes in bad weather with worthless drunk copilots, and I was even getting used to having de-ice costs taken out of my paycheck, but this was crossing the line. If I had somewhere else to go; I'd quit right now, but I didn't have anywhere to go. At this point, I'd sent my resume to just about every airline in the country, and I'd gotten the same response from all of them; "We've got x number of pilots on furlough right now, and we won't be hiring till all of them are called back." It could be years till anyone's hiring again.

Maybe Karen was right, *aviation is a dying industry*. It's definitely a dying career path anyway.

As for right now, all I could do was keep myself as far removed from The Chief's drug trafficking ring as possible. I even started to check all the work on my normal runs, just in case there were any illicit substances hidden in there. I wouldn't be surprised to find out that bags of checks were being used as decoys, I mean, who knew what The Chief was up to anymore. I also let some of the other captains know what was going on, and advised them to check their work and watch their asses as well.

It seemed as though my concerns put me in the minority around here though. Everyone was all jacked up that we had some new business, and not many people seemed too bothered by the type of business. In fact, some were even touting this to be the future of the company. "This is just the type of customer that could carry us into the next decade and beyond," I'd heard someone say.

It's like I was in the twilight zone.

The Co was so excited, that he decided to fill everyone he knew in on the details of what he now referred to as; "my new run." You would think he would want to keep this as quiet as possible, but if he wanted to shout it from the roof tops, well— I guess that's his journey. Personally, I felt that the less I knew the better, but The Co just wouldn't shut up about it.

"We will be flying under the cover of night." He told me. "We are already flying at night, so nobody will ever suspect a thing. Its genius, don't you think?"

"Oh yeah," I said. "I'm surprised no one has ever thought to try this before."

He then went on to tell me that; in four days, he, and the captain who had agreed to fly the drug run with him, were to fly out to some remote location that would be disclosed at the last minute, using a hand-drawn map as a guide. By following the streets and the landmarks that were on the map that the drug dealers would provide them, they were to find the approximate location of the pickup zone.

Once they found the pickup zone, they were to begin circling and flashing their lights. When the people on the ground spotted them, they would illuminate a field with the headlights from their cars, marking the landing area. "Sounds exciting, doesn't it?" The Co remarked.

"Sounds like prison time." I responded.

"Don't be jealous."

"Why would I be jealous? Remember, The Chief asked me to do this first, and I told him no."

Unable to find a comeback to this, The Co continued to tell me that; after landing, the plane would be loaded up with the drugs, and they would then be given a map revealing the location of the drop-off point. "Plus, I requested a few joints for the road," The Co added.

"Good idea." I remarked.

They would then depart and fly directly to the drop-off location. The entire flight was to be conducted at low altitude at night, flying over rural areas so as to not attract attention, "and we'll avoid any radar coverage areas." The Co added.

"Do you have any idea how to avoid radar coverage?" I asked. "Do you even know what radar is?"

"Well, no, but if I see any radar, I'll make sure we steer clear."

I nodded. "Sounds like it's gonna be a smashing success."

Four days later, the time for the drug run had come, and I still couldn't believe that this was really happening. Knowing The Co's reputation, I was sure it would be a disaster. And I couldn't believe it when The Co actually arrived to the airport on time. On top of that, he was on his best behavior.

I almost didn't recognize him when he strolled in at nine p.m. sharp wearing clean clothes. "Are you on time?" I asked him, checking to make sure my watch didn't stop.

"Yup, and I'm not drunk either." He said, "Just a little buzzed."

"Wow that's a first!"

I thought that I had seen it all. Then, for the first time ever, The Co contributed to the workload. He was actually helping out with the pre-flight. "Gotta make sure this bird's ready to go. This is the big leagues." He told me, as he opened the oil door on top of the left engine cowling, and without removing the dipstick, began pouring a quart of oil all over the top of the engine block.

As I watched the oil spilling out of the bottom of the cowling, all over the ramp, I informed him that, "This is not the big leagues. This is Busch league, and you're a freakin' idiot."

I was on standby that night, so once the flight departed; I hung out in the dispatch office, waiting for The Co to call from jail.

A couple hours later, it was much to my surprise to find out that the pickup went as planned. They had found the location of the pickup zone using the map they were given and landed in the field lit up by car's headlights. The plane was loaded up, The Co got his tip, and they were given the map that would lead them to the drop area.

After they departed, the drug dealers actually called The Chief and remarked that they were impressed with The Co and his captain's professionalism. That's a compliment The Co had never received before and would never receive again.

But just as I thought that The Co might actually pull this off, a call came in that the drop had not gone so well.

They had found the drop location using the hand-drawn map, and after flashing their lights, spotted the lit landing area. The captain lined the plane up with the landing area and began his descent. However, descending into the field in the dark, they did not realize how close they were to a tree line.

By the time they saw the trees approaching in their landing lights, it was too late. Just seconds before touching down their right wing clipped a tree, sending the plane cart-wheeling towards the ground. When the plane impacted the terrain, it burst into flames.

The Co and his captain struggled to escape the burning, twisted wreckage. Lucky for them, they were able to escape before the flames reached the cockpit. They walked away from the wreck without any serious injury, suffering only minor bumps and bruises. However, the airplane and its cargo were destroyed in the post-impact fire.

There's an old saying in aviation regarding fuel planning; it says that, "The only time you have too much fuel is when you're on fire."

Well, in this case that saying didn't hold true. It was a good thing they had so much fuel: the plane and cargo burned for hours rendering it unrecognizable and destroying all of the evidence.

All of the paperwork and anything that may have linked the plane to The Co, his captain, or Checkflight was gone. The Co and his captain were able to escape into the woods and hitchhike home. When the drug pickup team got to the plane and found that their precious cargo had been destroyed, they fled the scene as well.

The plane burned through the night and into the early morning hours without attracting any attention. No one ever reported the accident because the only witnesses were those who were involved. Someday the burnt wreckage would be discovered, which would most likely spark an investigation that would never be solved.

The Co and his captain got away scot-free. No legal action would ever be taken against them. The Chief and Checkflight, however, did not fare so well.

The drug dealers were not going to let this go. They demanded that The Chief reimburse them for their lost product. The Chief was forced to sell another one of our airplanes to pay them back, leaving us down two airplanes because of this whole thing. The Chief would also have to fake-sell the crashed airplane in order to get it off the books, so it would not one day raise questions.

A few days later I passed The Chief in the hall.

"Good call on the new business," I said as he passed.

The Chief didn't respond. I'm sure he was on his way to his office to come up with the next plan.

"We're going to be flying cash down to the Cayman Islands!" The Chief proclaimed, obviously thrilled with his new idea.

"What?" I questioned. "Money laundering?"

"Sort of."

"No, I'm not doing it."

"Just listen to the plan," The Chief continued, "it's genius. You will be flying down to Grand Cayman with cargo on board but there will also be extra packages that you will drop into the ocean before you get there. A boat will be waiting to pick them up. So, when you get there, you will clear customs with your perfectly legal cargo."

"And what about the boat?" I asked.

"It will be a fishing boat. No one will check it. They will leave from Georgetown Harbor in the morning to fish. When the time comes for the drop, they'll move into position, pick up the packages, and then return to the harbor seemingly after a day of fishing. They won't have to go through customs. Besides, even if they get busted, it's out of our hands at that point."

"What if they do get busted? You don't think people might try to find out how the money got in the ocean?"

"Maybe, but how could they link it to us?"

"Well, I'm still not doing it. Your little drug run was a disaster, and I don't see this going much better."

Of course, The Co jumped on board for this. While he wasn't quite as excited as he was for the drug run, it didn't take much for The Chief to talk him into it.

"I'll give you an extra fifty bucks to buy some duty-free rum while you're down there," The Chief told The Co.

"Deal!" The Co responded.

The Co then recruited the same captain who had flown the drug run with him. It seems that he had also not yet learned his lesson. And I was starting to think that nobody around here would quit until they were in jail.

Once again, everyone around here was excited about

Checkflight's new business venture. And upon reminding them of the recent failure of the drug run, the general response of most was, "yeah but this is so simple, how could it possibly go wrong?"

My thoughts were, "how could it go right?" Nothing around here ever goes as planned, and there were several things that would have to fall in place for this to work properly. Most importantly, the packages had to be dropped at the proper spot. The accuracy of our outdated navigation equipment was uncertain at best, making it highly unlikely the drop-zone could be properly located out on open waters that were devoid of visual landmarks.

The Chief did recognize this issue, and to my surprise, he bought a GPS specifically for this flight. While this may not seem like a big deal to most people, to us it was a historical event, seeing as that it was the first new piece of avionics equipment purchased by Checkflight in thirty-two years.

The Chief then locked himself in his office with the new GPS and spent several days struggling to figure out how to use it. Ultimately, he gave up, returned to the store where he bought it, and asked the clerk to program in the latitude and longitude coordinates of the location where the boat would be waiting. This ensured that the money would be dropped in the correct spot.

The next complication that The Co and his captain would have to deal with was the over-flight of Cuba. Cuba will permit American aircraft to over-fly their country, but they required forty-eight hours advance notice, and you must fly through a specific over-flight corridor at the exact time you requested in your application. I had my doubts on The Co's ability to pull this off.

The Co had to be on time for the flight's departure; otherwise, they may not make it to the over-flight corridor at the proper time. If they were late, they would be denied over-flight privileges, and be forced to fly an out-of-the-way route around Cuban airspace. The main problem with this being that any route, other than the initially planned route, would cause them to approach Grand Cayman on a course that would not over-fly the planned drop zone. If this happened, any unexplained request to then deviate back towards the drop zone would surely be met with suspicion from Cayman air traffic control.

The live-leg of the money laundering flight was to depart from Naples, Florida in the early morning, and while the promise of free weed had motivated The Co to be on time for the drug run, even The Chief wasn't sure if a few bottles of rum would provide enough encouragement for The Co to maintain this schedule. So, to ensure that the departure to Grand Cayman would be on time, The Chief decided to accompany The Co and his captain on the flight from Ohio down to Naples. And by "accompany" what he actually meant was; he would buy a ticket on a commercial airline and meet up them in Naples. He claimed the reason for this to be irritable bowel syndrome. "I can't go that long in a plane without a lav," he said, but I wasn't buying it. The Chief chose to ride on another airline because he knew better than to entrust his life on the reliability of one of Checkflight's airplanes.

The Chief made sure they left Naples on time, and it was now in The Co and his captain's hands to complete the mission. They departed for Grand Cayman, carrying a few hundred pounds of legal-looking fake checks to use as a decoy. This is what they would show the Cayman customs agents upon arrival. The real cargo was several hundred pounds of cash packed into four bundles that they would be dropping into the ocean off the coast of Grand Cayman prior to landing.

Thanks to The Chief's oversight of their timely departure, the over-flight of Cuba took place without any trouble. They hit the proper time window and contacted Havana Approach who cleared them for the over-flight of Cuban airspace.

Once they were past Cuba, it was time to prepare the packages for the drop. It was important for them to drop the packages in the proper location, about fifty miles off shore from Grand Cayman, and they would have to do this without slowing down or circling, which would surely arouse suspicion from Cayman Approach Control.

Upon spotting the boat, The Co was to inflate a floatation device that was attached to each package and then throw the package from the plane which would still be traveling at cruise speed. The packages would have to be dropped quickly once the boat was sighted to ensure none of them were lost at sea. They only had one shot at getting this right. Landing in Cayman with the money still on board was not an option.

"The GPS shows we're twenty miles from the drop zone. Go back and open the door," the captain said.

The Co climbed over the cargo net and made his way over the mountain of work towards the aft cargo door. The captain, who was flying the airplane, anxiously watched the distance to the drop zone waypoint count down on the GPS. "Ten miles," he announced, and he began looking for the recovery boat.

There was a problem though. Nobody had ever tested to see if the door could be opened under the aerodynamic forces of flight. The door was never designed to be opened in flight, and The Co quickly found that opening it, in opposition to the high-speed air flow that practically seized the locking pins in place, was not going to be easy. "I can't move the latch!" The Co yelled. "It's stuck!"

"Jump on it or something!" the captain suggested. "Five Miles, hurry!"

The Co stood up and slammed his foot down on the latch; it moved a little. He stomped on it again and it moved a little more.

"Two miles," the captain yelled.

No one had accounted for the possibility of the door not opening, and there was no back up plan at this point. They sure as hell couldn't land in Cayman with the money still on board. The Co at least knew that much, and realizing that his free rum was about to slip through his fingers, he began repeatedly stomping the latch as hard as he could, till ... The door finally flung open just in time for the captain to yell, "We're here! There's the boat! Start throwing!"

A rush of wind filled the cabin.

The Co hastily pulled the ripcord on the first package, inflating the floatation device and threw it. He then inflated and threw the second, followed by the third. But just as he was about to inflate the fourth one, the cargo door started to separate from the hinges. The front hinge's pin snapped and the door was now hanging on by just the rear hinge.

The captain yelled, "The doors about come off!"

The Co moved quickly and grabbed hold of the door handle. He struggled to steady the door with one hand as he reached for the fourth package with the other hand. But even stretching as far as he could, the package was out of his reach. At the speed they were traveling, they were getting farther away from the boat every second. If The Co didn't get the last package out quickly, the boat might not be able to find it.

"Hurry up, we're getting too far!" the captain yelled, "Throw it!"

The Co let go of the door which began violently fluttering in the wind. He grabbed the last package and pulled it towards him while trying to grab hold of the door handle again, but he couldn't reach it. The door ripped right off the second hinge and separated from the airplane hitting the tail before tumbling to the ocean.

"Throw it!" the captain yelled again.

In a panic, The Co let the last package go without inflating the floatation device. It dropped like a rock into the ocean and quickly sank.

The Co climbed back up to the cockpit. "Well, the packages are out," he told the captain, "but the door came off."

"Yeah, I don't know how we're going to explain this," the captain said, "but at least all the packages got dropped."

"Yeah," The Co said, failing to mention that the last one sunk.

During the next fifteen minutes before landing, they decided that they would tell customs that their door latch had failed shortly after departing Naples.

"The cargo door separated from the aircraft just off the coast of Florida," the captain said to the customs agent, "but we decided to continue the flight anyway because there was no safety hazard and our cargo has important deadlines."

Amazingly, the Cayman customs agents bought this story. They inspected the decoy cargo, searched the rest of the airplane and found nothing wrong. The customs agents released the decoy cargo to the decoy couriers who were waiting, pretending to be in a hurry to get the fake checks to the bank.

The captain called The Chief to inform him that the drop had been a success. "Well, other than the lost door and dented tail," he said, "but with the money we made from this we can easily replace the door."

"Actually, we can't," The Chief said. "The customer just called me. I already know about the door because they have it on their boat. They just told me that they are keeping the door, along with the rest of the airplane because you did not inflate the last package, and it sank. Is this true?"

"No," the captain said, "The Co inflated all the packages."

"Hey Co," the captain said to The Co who was already ordering a drink from the airport bar, "you inflated all the packages, right? 'Cause the customer is claiming that the last one sank."

"Uh, no I didn't inflate the last one," The Co said. "It sunk."

"Why didn't you inflate it?"

"Cause I was struggling to hold onto the door. You yelled 'just throw it'. I panicked and let the package go without inflating it."

"God damn it! Why didn't you tell me?"

"I didn't think it mattered. We got three out of four. So, they lost one."

"It was millions of dollars! They want to keep the airplane now!"

"Well, if they're keeping the airplane how are we going to get home?"

"Chief," the captain said into the phone, "The Co wants to know how we are going to get home."

The Chief, who had overheard the whole conversation said, "Well, I guess you two will have to buy yourselves a ticket on another airline."

"What? We don't have money for that."

"Then, I guess you'll just have to stowaway in someone's luggage or something, either way, I expect you back at work by tomorrow."

"But—" Before the captain could get another word in, The Chief hung up.

The captain turned to The Co. "He's said we've gotta find our own way home."

"Alright, that's fine," The Co said, "but, before we leave, I'm gonna go get my duty-free rum."

- 9 -
The One Gallon Challenge

Just days after the money laundering disaster the entire pilot group was asked to come in for an emergency meeting. Everyone was nervous. There was a rumor going around that some pilots would be furloughed, and I think we all knew that was a real possibility. Things hadn't been going well around here lately. Checkflight had been hemorrhaging business, and due to recent incidents, we were now down four airplanes. The Chief was trying to blame the declining economy for our troubles, but I knew this was all his fault.

When I pulled into the parking lot at Checkflight, the thought crossed my mind that maybe this was trap. Perhaps the feds had found out about The Chief's recent business experiments, and they were calling all of the pilots in here for questioning.

I'm innocent, I told myself. They can't pin any of that stuff on me. At least not the drug trafficking and money laundering, but as for breaking FAA regulations; I think every pilot here was guilty of that. It had become impossible to go a day of work here without breaking the regs.

I saw Rick's car in the parking lot, and decided I should call him before I went in. If it was a trap, hopefully he could tip me off before

I walked into it.

Rick answered. "What it be like man?"

"Hey, are you inside" I asked.

"At Checkflight?"

"Yeah."

"Yeah, I'm here."

"Are the Feds there? Cough if they are."

"No, the Feds aren't here, but I think some pilots are about to get canned. The Chief wants everyone in his office."

"Alright, I'll be in there in a minute."

Even though Rick had told me the coast was clear, I was still nervous when I entered the building. Every corner I turned on the way to The Chief's office, I was looking over my shoulder.

The Chief had us all pile into his tiny office and shut the door.

"The reason I called you all in today," The Chief began, "is because we need to make some cuts immediately. The company is in trouble, and if I don't get some people off the payroll quick, we're going to go bankrupt. As many of you may know, we've had the bad fortune to lose a few of our airplanes this week."

This made me laugh. *Bad fortune?*

The Chief continued, "I've already told Tony in maintenance that he is being let go."

I interrupted. "What? But Tony is the only mechanic we have. Who's going to do our maintenance?"

"Well, no one," The Chief said, "I'm cutting maintenance completely; we can't afford it anymore. You all can work on your own planes yourselves if you want to."

"But none of us are qualified," I said.

"Hey, tough times call for tough measures."

"Bullshit!" Rick coughed under his breath.

"And what about the Camaro Tug?" I asked.

"Tony will be taking it with him. You'll all just have to push your planes in and out of the hanger by hand from now on."

"You've gotta be kidding me." One of the pilots said.

"I'm not," The Chief said.

"Aren't you worried that Tony will murder your family?" I asked.

"Well, I don't have a family; so ... no." The Chief answered. "Anyway, to continue, I'm also letting Karen from dispatch go as well. Barbara will be taking over her shifts."

"Uhh, but we only have the two dispatchers as it is," I said. "How is this going to work? Barbara is already working twelve hours a day, seven days a week. What, is she going to work twenty-four seven?"

"Yes," The Chief answered.

"So, when is she going to sleep?" I asked.

"Hey, we all have to make a few sacrifices. Barbara will be fine. I'm sure she'll be happy about this news. She's better off than Karen who is losing her job altogether, don't you think?"

"Good point," The Co said.

"That's not a good point, you ass!" I yelled. "How is one ninety-year old senile woman going to run the dispatch department twenty-four hours a day seven days a week without ever having time to sleep? She doesn't even know where she is at most of the time!"

"Barbara has been in dispatch a long time," The Chief said. "She knows what she's doing."

"Bullshit!" Rick coughed under his breath again.

I gave up; it was useless to argue anymore; The Chief was intent on running this company on zero staff and there was no stopping him. And now he was taking advantage of a poor old woman who would never know any better.

"If we're done talking about Barbara, I'll move on," The Chief continued. "The reason I called all of you in today was to inform you that a pilot will have to be cut too."

"God damn it!" Rick blurted out, "Who?"

The Chief turned to address Rick, "Well Rick, the good news is it's not you. Chip and The Co are the lowest on the seniority list and have equal seniority, as far as I can tell, because they were hired at the same time."

Rick asked, "How can two people have equal seniority?"

"Because, they were never officially issued sonority numbers when they were hired, and it's too late to do anything about that now."

This was typical of Checkflight. While most airlines have a highly structured seniority system, that becomes thee deciding factor in the event of a furlough; at Checkflight seniority was handled in just as disorganized a fashion as everything else at this company.

"That's ridiculous," I said. "Chip what's your seniority number?"

"I don't know," Chip said. "I never got one."

Figures.

"Co?" I asked.

"Huh?" The Co muttered.

"Never mind," if The Co was ever issued a seniority number at all, I'm sure he forgot it seconds later.

"Don't worry," The Chief said. "I've already come up with a plan to settle the tie breaker."

"How's that?" Chip asked.

"The only way to settle this fairly is by holding a One Gallon Challenge." The Chief's eyes lit up when he said this, as if he'd been waiting for this day for years.

Chip asked, "What's a One Gallon Challenge?"

The Chief explained, "You and The Co will each be given a gallon of Mexican tap water. Both of you will begin chugging it at the same time. The first person to vomit, shit themselves, lose consciousness, or die will be furloughed. The other will then be crowned the champion of The One Gallon Challenge and keep their job."

Every pilot in the room stood in shock, even for The Chief, this was pretty far out there. I had to say something about this. "Don't you think that's a little insensitive? I mean, someone is about to lose their job and you're going to humiliate them as well?"

"I feel that the One Gallon Challenge is fair system, and I stand by my decision." The Chief proclaimed.

"Bullshit," Rick coughed under his breath again.

"Where the hell are you getting Mexican tap water in Ohio?" I asked.

"I keep several gallons at home on reserve for just such occasions," The Chief answered.

"When are we doing this?" Chip asked.

"The One Gallon Challenge will be held tomorrow at high noon out in the parking lot," The Chief responded. "Anyone that wants to come watch is welcome."

"You're inviting a crowd to watch? You're making this a spectator sport? This is barbaric!" I said angrily.

"No, it's fair!" The Chief shot back. "Just be glad you're not the one on the cutting block!"

"For now," I mumbled.

The Chief glared at me, "What's that? Care to speak up?"

"Nothing, never mind." I said.

The Chief's face flushed red, he pointed his finger at me and began screaming, "Better be nothing, 'cause to tell you the truth if we didn't have this stupid seniority system, you'd be the first to go! You know, you've been real a pain in the ass lately, always complaining and refusing duty assignments. You should learn to be a little more like your first officer," he pointed to The Co, "he's a model employee, a real company man I can always count on no matter what the mission may be."

I spoke up. "Your so called 'model employee' was personally responsible for the loss of one of your airplanes a few days ago, and he played a major role in the loss of a couple others. If you call that a company man; I don't know what to tell you."

The Chief shot back. "At least he tried to complete the mission! And that's a hell of a lot more than I can say for you! He didn't just sit there— and whine— like you've been spending most of your time doing lately!" he launched into a whiney impression of me, "'I need a de-ice. The plane's broke and it's not safe to fly. The cargo's illegal' … Sound familiar?"

Listening to this, I had a flashback to the day I was hired here "safety is always our number one priority," The Chief told me back then. So much has changed, not that safety was ever really the number one priority around here, but these days it's not even anywhere near being on the list of priorities of this company.

These days, people that are willing to do anything regardless of the consequences, people like The Co; who show up to work drunk, and are more than willing to partake in drug trafficking; those are the model employees, and I don't belong here.

"Yeah, that sounds about right." I said.

The Chief appeared satisfied that he had made his point. "Great! So … Chip … Co, your fate will be determined at high noon tomorrow. And as for the rest of you, don't get too excited about keeping your jobs." He warned the crowd, "only one pilot will be let go tomorrow, but there will be plenty more to follow," as if we needed a reminder that at any moment, we could all be unemployed.

The room fell silent for a minute till The Chief broke the silence by telling us all to get out of his office. "That'll be it; you all can go now," he shooed us out.

As the pilots all filed out of The Chief's office, The Co whispered to me, "What did he say? I spaced out there for a few minutes."

"You weren't listening?"

"Naw, I wasn't paying attention."

"You may be losing your job!" I told him. "You have to be here tomorrow at high noon for some sort of Mexican water showdown!"

"Alright, alright, calm down," The Co said, "I'll be here."

The following morning a large crowd assembled in the Checkflight parking lot. There must have been a few hundred people there. People brought their brothers, cousins, friends of friends of friends, and everyone was there to witness The One Gallon Challenge. Bookies took bets on who would win, and people even wore homemade shirts declaring their favored champion.

Just about everyone in town was there, that is, except for The Co; he was late like usual.

A few minutes past high-noon the Chip argued for a forfeit, citing his better work ethic. "I actually showed up," he said frustrated. "The Co's not even here."

The Chief wouldn't budge though. He stood atop a make-shift platform, that he most likely stayed up all night constructing, and addressed the audience through a bull horn. "Folks, there will be a One Gallon Challenge today!" he assured them. "That is how the victor will be decided!" He then lowered the bull horn and quietly said to Chip, "I'm not going to start firing people just because they don't show up on time."

But as the clock ticked by and The Co had not shown yet, the crowd grew increasingly impatient. People had come here to witness a spectacle. If the One Gallon Challenge did not start soon, a riot was liable to break out.

"Let's torch this place!" someone instigated.

"Sir, please do not insight a riot," The Chief said, "I assure you The Co is on his way." But The Chief didn't know that for sure, and the mob disregarded his plea for order. A group of people picked up a car and carried it into the grassy area next to the parking lot.

For all we knew The Co was probably blacked out in a ditch somewhere.

Out of fear that my car would be the next one to be carried away, I tried calling The Co's cell, but it went straight to voicemail. I left a message, "Man, you better get here quick! Things are getting out of hand."

Then, at twelve forty-nine, just before all hell broke loose, The Co's car came tearing into the parking lot. "It's The Co, he's here!" someone yelled.

"Great," Chip mumbled. He had been hoping that The Co would never show so he could win by default.

A group of people that had been attempting to roll over a squad car gently set it back down and rejoined the rest of the audience.

When The Co opened his car door to get out, a glass bottle rolled out and shattered on the pavement. Everyone watched as he used his foot to quickly shuffle the glass towards a nearby storm drain.

"I'm here, I'm here," The Co said as he approached the awaiting crowd. "I got pretty dinged up last night. I woke up late, sorry." He climbed atop the platform where The Chief and Chip were waiting.

"That's alright, you're here now," The Chief said to him.

The Chief then raised the bull horn to his mouth, "The One Gallon Challenge will now begin!"

The crowd cheered. "Go Co!" one of them shouted. "Chip's my hero," yelled another.

The Chief walked up to The Co and Chip, handing them each a one-gallon milk jug filled with dingy yellowish looking water. One last time, he reviewed the rules, "First one to puke, shit, pass out, or die will be furloughed! May the best man win!"

"What happens if we both finish the whole gallon?" Chip asked.

"I wouldn't worry about that." The Chief said to him. "But, if that does happen, we will all wait here for one of you to flush out."

"Okay," Chip said, "let's get this over with."

The Chief then raised a starting pistol into the air. "Ready?"

The crowd fell silent as The Co and Chip both removed the caps from their jugs and brought them to their lips. "Ready," they both responded.

"Go!" The Chief yelled as he fired the pistol in the air.

The One Gallon Challenge was underway as the two of them tipped their jugs back and began taking slugs of the foul water...

About three seconds later... The One Gallon Challenge was over.

Chip's flow reversed almost immediately after taking his first drink.

"Shit, why did I bet on Chip?" someone yelled from the audience, "I should have known he had a weak stomach."

Money began to change hands throughout the crowd as Chip puked on his shoes.

"The victor has been decided!" The Chief announced, "The Co is the champion!"

The audience wailed with mixed boos and shouts of triumph.

The Chief lowered his bull horn, turned to Chip and said, "Chip, you're furloughed; please remove yourself from company property immediately."

Chip dropped his jug on the stage. It splashed and fell over on its side, spilling out the remains of the Mexican water. With his head hung low he climbed down from the platform and sauntered to his busted-up car, pausing every few steps to vomit.

The Co, however, was still drinking the water.

"Stop drinking that," I told him, "the contest is over. You're gonna be shitting through a screen door for a week."

"But I'm thirsty," The Co said. It appeared that the Mexican water was not fazing him a bit. I guess his stomach was used to all sorts of horrible things.

The Chief addressed the audience. "Folks I'd like to thank you all for attending the first running of The Checkflight One Gallon Challenge. There will be plenty more furloughs, so come back and see us again... And now for the crowning of the champion!"

The crowd applauded, and The Chief then reached behind the platform, revealing a cardboard pirate's hat which he placed on The Co's head.

It was The Co's most shining moment. He set his jug down, turned to face the audience, and in a display of showmanship I was all too familiar with, he heaved his arms towards the sky, and screamed, "Viva la Checkflight!"

But it was his cardboard pirate's hat crown that really said it all. It read, "I threw boring overboard at Long John Silver's."

Later that night, while The Chief sat in his office, counting his winnings from the bets he had placed on The Co, the phone rang. He answered. "Hello."

"CHIEF!" Karen screamed into his ear. "Sherman's going to come down there and beat your ass! And he's an ultimate cage fighting champion! You're gonna be sorry you fired me!"

Then she hung up.

The Chief listened to the dial tone for a few seconds before setting the phone down. Moments later, the phone rang again. "What do you want Karen?" The Chief screamed into the receiver, "Sherman's not even real!"

"Ahh, sorry to bother you, sir," the man on the other end said, "but this is Tim from Orlando Executive Airport Authority. One of your airplanes just crashed into a hangar down here."

"What?"

"Yes sir, one of your planes just landed here a few minutes ago. The plane then came taxiing across the ramp at high speed, crashing into the hangar building. The pilot jumped out of the plane, ran to the parking lot, and fled the scene in a crew car."

"But none of our planes were going to Orlando tonight?"

"It was definitely your plane, sir." He gave The Chief the tail number of the plane. It was one of ours.

The Chief slammed the phone down and stormed down to the dispatch office.

Barbara was sitting in her cubicle playing bingo on her computer, "B1, B2!" she yelled as The Chief stormed in, "I don't have any of these! This is so stupid!" She threw her mouse at the computer monitor.

"Barbara!" he yelled, "who flew to Orlando tonight?"

"Chip," she said.

"But Chip was furloughed."

"Oh, yes, I forgot about that."

"You forgot?" The Chief was enraged. "How could you forget? It just happened today!"

"I forgot. Chip told me he was doing a special charter for you.

He left this note."

Barbara handed The Chief the note. As The Chief was opening it, Barbara asked, "Where is Karen?"

"Karen was fired."

"Why do you want to ruin everything?" Barbara screamed. "Why are you killing people!?"

"I'm not killing people Barbara. I just had to let some people go."

Barbara sat there with her arms crossed looking angrily at The Chief. He turned to leave. "Your sweater is stupid, and you are Satan!" she screamed, as he walked out the door.

Barbara may not have been "all there" anymore, but even she had enough sense to know that The Chief had destroyed this company.

The Chief went back to his office, sat down at his desk, and read the note.

"Dear Chief," it read, "I have nothing left to live for. My wife has taken a new lover, my car is totaled, and I've lost my job. I have been practicing my HALO skills, and I am going to Florida to try to win her back. Sorry about stealing the airplane. Chip"

Alex Stone

- 10 -
Don't Loop Your Money Maker

Checkflight was a company that stayed in business by keeping a low profile and not attracting attention. The Chief's One Gallon Challenge spectacle put a spotlight on us. We now had much more attention than we needed, and we were about to have more. There had been a ridiculous amount of shady activities going on around here lately, and somehow The Chief kept getting away with them. However, behind the scenes, the Feds were starting to take notice. Recently, several of our aircraft had either been destroyed or mysteriously written off the books, and FAA investigators wanted to know why. Though they were still not sure what we were up to, we were now on their radar.

Less than twenty-four hours after the furlough of Chip, Checkflight's lenders foreclosed on our operations building and the airport authority repossessed our hangar. The Chief was now operating the company out of a motor home that the airport authority was allowing him to park on the public ramp, along with the few airplanes we had left. I'm sure they figured it would only be for a few days.

With the promise of more furloughs on the way, and the very real possibility of this whole house of cards collapsing any day now, the pilots were growing increasingly disgruntled. Everyone was upset due to the recent firing of Karen and Tony, and especially the furlough of Chip, which The Chief had turned into his own personal money hungry circus. It had been yet another of our trusty leaders' sleazy attempts to bring in revenue, though it did little to stop the tailspin this doomed company was in. Since then several more routes had been canceled; in most cases with the customers either citing that they were "going digital and no longer had a need for our services," or were "switching to another (more reliable, more professional) carrier."

Checkflight was hanging on by a thread.

Early on a Sunday morning, The Chief called Rick into his office to inform him that the route that Rick normally flew on Tuesdays was being cut. This was the second work day Rick had lost in the past week; just days earlier he had been informed that the run he normally flew on Wednesdays had been cut. He had only been working four days a week as it was, and now, with the loss of two of those days, he would only be working two days a week.

"How do you expect me to pay my bills when I'm only working two days a week?" Rick asked The Chief.

"I don't know," The Chief said. "You're a big boy; figure it out."

Rick left the motor home bedroom that The Chief was now using as his office without saying another word. He passed through the motor home's living room that was now the dispatch office, where Barbara was playing online bingo, and walked out onto the public ramp towards his airplane.

Rick's co-pilot was there waiting for him. "Hey Rick, I pre-flighted the plane, but the left gear door won't close," his co-pilot said.

Upon hearing this and seeing the left gear door hanging open, Rick promptly got down under the wing of the Navajo on all fours. With his back to the hanging gear door, he began kicking it repeatedly in a furious attempt to shut it. His co-pilot watched in horror as Rick stomped the gear door with the bottom of his foot until its hydraulic strut snapped, leaving it completely broken, with no chance of closing ever again.

Rick stood up to inspect his handy work. The gear door still hung open, and now the broken hydraulic strut hung limp inside the wheel well. "Fuck it. Looks good to me," Rick said. "Let's go."

His copilot, sensing that Rick must've received more bad news, asked, "What'd The Chief have to say?"

"We lost our Tuesdays," Rick said.

"So now we just have two days a week?"

"Yup, Sunday and Monday's all we've got" Rick told him, as he climbed into the plane.

"That's bullshit!" his copilot said.

"Yup."

His co-pilot followed him into the plane, shutting the cabin door behind him. "Do you think any more days will be cut?" he asked.

Rick didn't respond. He was in no mood for talking.

As they taxied to the runway, his copilot held up the checklist and asked, "Do you want me to do the before takeoff checklist?"

"No," Rick said. He grabbed the checklist out of his copilot's hands and threw it over his shoulder to the back of the plane.

After that, his copilot remained silent through the takeoff and the first part of the flight. He could see that The Chief had obviously sent Rick over the edge.

Rick and his copilot were flying from our home base in nowhere, Ohio to Indianapolis. About thirty minutes into the flight, near the Indiana border, they ran into some rain showers. As Navajo's always do, the plane began to leak water into the cockpit. Rick watched for several minutes as water leaked in around the windshield frame and dripped on top of the glare-shield where it was pooling up.

Over several minutes, the puddles slowly grew larger and larger until they spilled over the edge of the glare-shield, dripping down onto Rick's knees.

Rick shook his head in disappointment. Reaching into the pocket on the back of his seat, he found the aircraft's flight manual and pulled it out. He randomly opened it and held it, pages up, under the dripping water. His co-pilot who took note of the fact that, Rick was using a legally required document to soak up water, spoke up. "What'cha up to?"

"My knees are getting wet; I'm soaking up the water." Rick said, matter-of-factly, as if there was nothing wrong with what he was doing. Then, the plane got hit by a jolt of turbulence, and Rick hit his head on a hanging piece of ceiling liner.

The ceiling liner right above Rick's seat had been falling off for months, and he had hit his head on the jagged piece of plastic several times, always laughing it off, but not today.

"God damn it!" he screamed. "I wish maintenance would fix this damn thing! Oh wait, I almost forgot. We don't have maintenance anymore!"

He dropped the flight manual, as the water leak was no longer his biggest problem. Then reached up and grabbed the hanging piece of ceiling liner and yanked on it, ripping it and half the ceiling down in one swipe.

Fiberglass insulation and pieces of broken plastic rained down in the cockpit. His co-pilot ducked away. "Dude, what are you doing?"

"Well, The Chief said we could fix things ourselves if we want to," Rick said, as he sat staring at the rather large chunk of ceiling that was in his hand.

His copilot didn't know what to say, he sat silently as Rick tossed the chunk of ceiling over his shoulder behind the seat.

Rick then launched into a violent rage, clawing and tearing at the ceiling, finishing the job he'd started by ripping down every little piece of ceiling liner that was still clinging on. He tossed each piece over his shoulder, and pulled out all of the insulation, leaving the ceiling bare metal.

When Rick finished with the ceiling his eyes began darting around the cockpit. He was brainstorming ideas to further damage the airplane. Then it hit him—burn the starters up. He grabbed a hold of left engine starter switch and began cranking it. The gears in the starter whined and ground as Rick cranked it.

After a minute, the noise stopped. His copilot stared in fear as Rick moved on to the right engine starter, cranking it until it quit too.

"There," Rick said in satisfaction, "now we're broke down at the next stop. Once we shut these engines down, they ain't restarting. Maintenance will have to replace these starters if they want this thing to fly again. Oh wait, we don't have maintenance anymore. Too bad."

Rick's copilot remained quiet until they landed in Indy. After shutting the engines down, Rick checked the starters to be sure they were both inop. The left one made a whining noise but the prop didn't turn; the right one did nothing.

"Well we're definitely broke," Rick said. "I guess I'll call Barbara." He pulled out his cell phone and dialed.

"Dispatch, this is Barbara," she answered.

"Hey Barbara, it's Rick."

"Rick who?" she asked.

"Rick the pilot who works there. I just saw you an hour ago when I left."

"I thought your name was Tim."

"No Barbara, that's someone else; this is Rick."

"Oh yes. Rick. How can I help you?"

"We're broke down."

"Oh no, what happened?"

"Both starters are broke," Rick told her. "The plane won't start."

"Oh boy, I just don't know what to do. Let me ask The Chief. I'm going to put you on hold for a minute."

"Okay Barbara."

A few moments later, Barbara was back.

"Tim," Barbara said, "The Chief would like to speak with you; here he is."

"It's Rick."

"What? Rick who?"

"Never mind," Rick said.

Barbara transferred the call from the motor home living room to the motor home bedroom.

"Hello," The Chief answered.

"Hey, it's Rick."

"Oh Rick, I thought it was Tim," The Chief said. "Anyway, what's this Barbara tells me? Both your starters are inop."

"Yup," Rick said, "it won't turn over at all."

"Well, how did that happen?"

"I don't know; the plane's a piece of shit."

"Well, did you try hand propping it?"

"Hell no!" Rick said. "I'm not hand propping it!"

"I'm not saying you have to do it." The Chief said, "look around, see if you can find someone standing around that looks disposable and have them hand prop it for you."

"Chief, I don't see any disposable people standing around."

"Well, what about your co-pilot?" The Chief asked, "You could finish the run without him. Couldn't you?"

"I'm not going to sacrifice my co-pilot to finish the run!" Rick screamed, "You can send us another airplane or were not going anywhere!"

"Ugh, fine, let me see what I can do. I'll call you back."

Over the next twenty minutes The Chief called Rick back several times, each time attempting to convince him to find "a disposable human being" to hand prop the Navajo. But Rick continually refused, and hung up. Eventually, The Chief caved and had two standby pilots fly a plane out to Indy so Rick could finish his route.

When he got off the phone, his co-pilot asked, "What's going on?"

"The Chief's got another crew bringing us a new airplane. He said they'll be here in an hour."

Rick jumped down from the wing where he had been sitting and opened the rear cargo door on the now immobile Navajo. He removed two slips of paper from plastic sleeves that were attached to the wall just inside the door.

"What are you doing with those?" his co-pilot inquired, referring to the Navajo's airworthiness and registration certificates that Rick was strolling away with.

Rick headed for the FBO, and without looking back, he said, "I've gotta take a deuce; I need something to wipe my ass with."

About three hours later, once Rick had a fresh airplane, he and his copilot departed for their last stop of the day, which was Chicago

Midway. They had their company-issued tent on board, and were planning on pitching it in the Midway Airport parking lot, where they would be spending the night.

When they leveled off in cruise, Rick was already brainstorming ideas to break this plane. But he came up with something better. "I'm going to enter an air show," Rick announced to his copilot.

"What? In what airplane?" his copilot asked.

"This one."

"Who's gonna go to an air show to see a busted-up old cargo plane?"

"I bet people will enjoy it," Rick said. "In fact, it'll probably make the show. I bet we even make the news."

"Wait, *we?*"

"Yeah we," Rick said, pointing back and forth between the two of them. "The Chicago Air and Water Show is going on right now, and that's where we're headed."

Rick's copilot started to realize that he was serious. "Don't do it!" he said, "and if you do, I want no part of it."

"That's fine. I'll tell everyone you tried to stop me."

"Well, what are you planning to do?"

"A loop right over Navy Pier," Rick proclaimed.

"I don't think this thing will even do a loop."

"It will," Rick said. "I'll make it loop."

"You know you're gonna get busted. I doubt you'll be able to get away with it."

"It'll be worth it. I don't really want to fly anymore anyway."

"Why not?"

"Cause this job sucks," Rick said, "and no one else is hiring. My aviation record is already tarnished; I've got no future as a pilot, so I'm gonna do something else with my life."

"Like what?"

"I still don't know, but I'm definitely not going to work anywhere that requires sleeves!"

"Hum?" There was a pause for a moment while his co-pilot thought about this, then he suggested, "Aren't you obsessed with lawn equipment? Why don't you become a landscaper or a gardener or something?"

A light bulb illuminated over Rick's head. "You know, that's a pretty good idea. Landscapers never wear sleeves, and they work outside. I like it!" He paused for a moment. "Anyway, I might as well finish my aviation career with a bang. So, I'm doing a loop in the air show."

"You're crazy."

"Well, what about you? What are you going to do when Checkflight goes under?"

"I don't know. I've been trying not to think about it. But, I'm pretty sure Checkflight won't make it through the week. I mean we're using a motor home as our headquarters."

"Yeah, and I'm pretty sure The Chief is living in that thing," Rick added, "it looks like he's got all his stuff in that bedroom he's using as an office."

"I *kinda* was wondering the same thing. I bet he had to sell his house to buy it."

"Probably," Rick agreed.

"I just don't know man; I mean, I probably won't find another job in aviation for a long time. Maybe, it is time to go in another direction."

"Well come on then," Rick said, "let's go in a different direction. And if The Chief wants the final days of Checkflight to be a circus, like his little One Gallon Challenge, let's make it a circus. Let's humiliate him before he has the chance to humiliate us."

Rick reached down in his flight bag and rummaged around for a minute, eventually digging out a pill bottle. He opened the cap and dumped two small pills out on his hand. "I've got two left," he said, "one for you, one for me."

"What are they?" his co-pilot asked.

"Prednisone … two-point-five milligrams … Steroids."

"Are you crazy?"

Rick grabbed his co-pilot's hand, cupped it, and dropped one of the pills into his palm. He took the other pill, popped it in his own mouth, swallowed, and said, "Come on dude, screw Checkflight. Let's go out with a bang."

His co-pilot stared at the pill that was in his hand for a moment. He took a deep breath. "Alright, let's do it. I'm in." he said, and he abruptly grabbed the Navajo's maintenance log, set it flat on his lap, smashed the pill on it with his flashlight, and snorted it.

"Holy shit!" Rick was shocked.

"This job sucks. Let's loop this thing!" his co-pilot screamed with his arm outstretched.

"That's the spirit, now nix those sleeves!"

Rick's co-pilot grabbed a handful of his left sleeve, tugged at it and ripped it off right at the seams. He tossed the dead sleeve to the floor, and then repeated by ripping off his right sleeve, also pitching it down on the moldy carpet.

Rick looked down at his co-pilot's lifeless former arm coverings that now lay on the floor, soaking up pooled rain water. It was a proud moment. "Congratulations on becoming a juice-head." Rick said, and held his fist up to his co-pilot. "Bump me."

His co-pilot bumped his fist, and instantly Rick pulled his hand back and spread his fingers slowly apart while making explosion sound effects.

"Checkflight 251, say altitude." Air traffic control cut in, interrupting the bromance.

In the midst of all the commotion, Rick had completely neglected to fly the airplane, which had now drifted away from their assigned cruising altitude due to an autopilot malfunction.

"Shit!" Rick said, "The autopilot quit." He keyed up the mic, "Checkflight 251, we're at six thousand six hundred, looks like our altitude hold quit on us."

"Yeah, 251 you were supposed to be maintaining seven thousand. Can you try to maintain that please?"

The controller spoke in a bitchy tone that Rick didn't care for. He made no attempt to return to his assigned altitude, nor did he respond to the controller.

A few moments later the controller inquired again, "Checkflight 251, do you copy maintain seven thousand?"

"Whatever," Rick responded.

"Excuse me?" the controller said.

"You heard me."

"Sir, are you going to maintain seven thousand or not? 'Cause if not, I'm going to have to issue you a violation."

Rick keyed up the mic, "Sir, are you wearing sleeves right now?"

"Excuse me?"

"You're not excused," Rick said, "I asked you if you're wearing sleeves right now."

"If you're asking if my shirt has sleeves; yes, it does … Tell you what Checkflight, I've got a phone number for you to copy down." The controller read off a phone number. "Give us a call when you get on the ground and we can discuss this."

"Alright," Rick said, "I look forward to speaking with you." He turned to his co-pilot, "Turn off the transponder, so they can't see our altitude anymore."

His co-pilot hesitated for a moment then said, "well, I guess I'm too far into this to turn back now," and he shut the transponder off.

The controller, who was undoubtedly in shock over this unprecedented insubordination, never made any mention of the loss of the transponder signal. I'm sure he was telling himself that, "it would probably be wise not further aggravate these maniacs."

Before long, Rick and his co-pilot were handed off to Chicago approach control who advised them to expect runway three-one center for landing.

"They've probably already got someone on the ground at Midway waiting for us," Rick said, "too bad we won't be landing there."

"Where are we going to land? I mean, after the loop," his co-pilot asked.

"Uhh … I think the best idea would be to put it down at some small uncontrolled airport; definitely someplace where we can get a taxi quick, so we can make a getaway … Actually, now that I think about it; I know a good spot, don't worry about it."

"Got'cha"

It was a perfectly clear sunny day in Chicago. "Perfect day for an air show," Rick said. "When ATC gives us a turn to final approach, I'm just going to ignore them and head straight for downtown."

And that's exactly what Rick did.

"Checkflight 251, how do you hear approach?" the controller asked when they didn't respond to their turn to final.

"Don't answer them," Rick said, as he aimed the plane straight for Navy Pier. "I'll fly the plane, you be the lookout. Let me know if you see any other planes near us, 'cause I don't want to cause a midair."

"So far, it looks clear." His co-pilot said.

"Checkflight 251, Chicago?" The controller was getting concerned now, or at least more concerned they he already was, since the previous controller had no doubt filled him in on Rick's questionable mental status. But Rick didn't answer. He pushed the nose over, descending at full throttle, picking up speed.

The decrepit Navajo buzzed over Grant Park where thousands of air-show spectators had gathered to watch high-tech fighter jets and aerobatic planes. Little did they expect to see this bucket.

"Looks clear," his copilot said, as they approached the lake shore. "I don't see any planes in the area."

Now just fifty feet above the water, barely higher than the masts on the hundreds of sail boats that filled Burnham Harbor, Rick was close enough to see the surprised expressions on the boater's faces. "Here we go!" He yelled, as he pulled the plane up into a vertical just as they passed in front of Navy Pier. But the airplane struggled and lost momentum quick.

The old cargo plane was heavy with cargo and light on horsepower. The airspeed rapidly declined, and the plane struggled to crest the top of the loop. It hung there for a moment that seemed like an eternity to Rick, till finally, the engines quit.

The fuel system wasn't designed for aerobatics, and the engines lost fuel pressure at such an extreme angle.

Now without power, the plane stalled inverted, and plummeted towards the lake. The work in the back of the plane tumbled and thrashed about. Rick hastily rolled the plane upright and put the nose down to regain speed and break the stall.

The stall broke, but the engines were out and they were too low. Rick quickly saw his only option was ditching. "Full flaps!" he yelled.

His co-pilot slammed the Navajo's flap handle down. The

airspeed slowed and waves kissed the underbelly of the plane. The engines sputtered a little, but it was too late. Rick pulled the fuel cut-offs just as the plane glided into the dark Lake Michigan water right in front of Soldier Field.

They hit the water, and the plane bounced violently nearly flipping over when a wing tip caught a wave.

When the plane settled to a stop, it began to sink. Rick and his copilot unbuckled their shoulder harnesses and climbed out of the airplane onto the wing. Within a minute, a coast guard boat pulled up next to them.

Rick and his copilot were pulled onto the boat just in time to watch the plane disappear below the surface.

The Feds jumped into action quick. They were at the scene before the boat even got to shore. The Feds love a good foul play story. Try to get them to show up on this short of notice for anything else.

"Are you two okay?" an FAA inspector asked Rick as he stepped out of the Coast Guard boat.

"Yeah, we're okay," Rick said.

"In that case, can I see your certificates?"

"Sure," Rick said pulling out his wallet, "we lost control of the plane. The flight controls jammed up."

"Then why didn't you respond to air traffic control?" the Fed asked.

"I freaked out. I didn't know what to do."

"Son," the inspector said, "you realize we already have the ATC transcripts and we're going to recover your cockpit voice recorder. Is that the story you want to stick with?"

"Alright," Rick said, "we tried to loop the plane on purpose."

As soon as Rick spoke those words, the inspector pulled a pair of scissors out of his pocket and began cutting Rick's pilot's license into pieces.

Rick watched the severed pieces of his former pilot's license drop to the ground. "Do you carry those scissors around all the time just for that?" he asked.

"You never know when just such an occasion will arise," the inspector said, as he tossed the last piece of Rick's license on the ground.

"Well whatever, I'm done with aviation anyway."

"And you," the inspector said to Rick's copilot, "did you have a part in this?"

"Yes sir," he responded.

"Fork it over."

I had been watching this scene unfold on CNN from my apartment. I watched as they handcuffed Rick and his co-pilot.

Just before loading them into a police car, a news reporter stuck a microphone in front of Rick.

News Reporter: *Sir, do have any comment, why did you do it?*
Rick: *'Cause I work for Checkflight.*

That was all he said. And with that, police officers shoved Rick into the back of their squad car and drove off.

I shut the TV off. *This was it*, I thought. The worst would be yet to come for Checkflight. For all the illegal things we'd done, including a drug run and money laundering. This stupid stunt was the one that would really get the FAA interested in us. If the Fed's weren't already hiding in the bushes with binoculars near Checkflight's motor home, gathering evidence and waiting for the right time to bring the hammer down, they would be soon. And once they start searching for accountability for the things they find, The Chief would take the first opportunity he got to ship *my* ass down the river.

I left my apartment to go to work. On the drive there, the more I thought about it, I needed to get out of this job. Staying here any longer could possibly ruin my entire aviation career. But, how could I get out? I still needed a job and if I quit I wouldn't qualify for unemployment. I had to be furloughed.

I decided that, upon arriving at the airport, I would beg The Chief to furlough me. That way I could collect unemployment for a few months, while I tried to find another job. It was a risky decision, as the aviation industry and the economy in general slipped further down the toilet. It was highly likely that I would be unable to find another job prior to my unemployment benefits running out, but it was the only choice I had.

The Chief couldn't have been happier. "That's great!" He said. "I was going to have to furlough someone else anyway; it's very noble of you to volunteer. But you do realize that you will still be subject to a One Gallon Challenge."

"What the fuck for!?" I questioned. "Who am I competing against?"

"No one. You'll just be competing against yourself. But I'll find a ringer for you to lose to; they'll just have regular water in their jug of course."

"Then what's the point? If no one else is on the chopping block, and I'm volunteering for furlough; why are you making me do this?"

"'Cause, I very much look forward to these One Gallon Challenges. It's a fun time for everyone, and it's the one good thing that has come from the hard times we're currently experiencing … and we can all make a little money on the side, ya know what I mean."

"But—"

"No one gets out of here without a One Gallon Challenge!" The Chief stated firmly.

"Fine, I'll do it. When?"

"Well, I still need you fly tonight, this will be your last night. When you get back here tomorrow morning, you'll drink the Mexican water till you puke, shit—"

I interrupted. "Yes, I know the rules."

"Good, then tomorrow morning you can eliminate yourself from the company by losing the One Gallon Challenge to yourself, and I will place you on the furlough list."

"Thank you." I said.

"And you better make your deadlines tonight; otherwise I might change my mind."

"Gotcha."

And with that I went outside to pre-flight, feeling relief that I was just one night of flying and one gallon of Mexican tap water away from freedom.

- 11 -
Run for the Fence

The Co and I were enroute to St. Louis Parks. We'd make a quick stop there, then another at Chicago Midway, and finally back to Ohio. It was my final night at Checkflight and I couldn't be happier about that, however just like every other night at this company my last would not be met without difficulty.

The weather was mostly clear in the St. Louis area, but there were some small patches of fog. When we were about forty miles out, I listened to the Parks Airport's automated weather forecast. The weather report showed calm winds and clear skies, but the visibility was less than a quarter mile due to low lying fog.

"Shit!" I said. "It's below minimums."

"What does that mean?" The Co asked.

"It means we can't land. We need at least a half mile visibility to legally land here. How do you not know this?"

"I just don't care."

"Then why did you ask?"

"I don't know, just making conversation," The Co said, as he went back to playing his Game Boy.

"Not caring; that's cool." I said. But while The Co wasn't much concerned about our little predicament, I on the other hand was. Especially since the fog would probably not lift until well after sunrise, and that was several hours away. I wanted to get this night over with as quickly as possible, and at the moment, the thought of having to wait in a holding pattern till the weather improved didn't much appeal to me. The real problem, however, was that even if I had been in the mood to kill some time in a hold, we didn't even have that option.

We were running out of gas. In fact, we were right on the verge of a fuel emergency, and it was all due to The Chief's latest cost cutting tactic.

Just a few days prior, The Chief had announced that he would no longer be allowing flight crews to decide for themselves how much fuel they would need for a flight. "Effective immediately," he had told us, "I will be allotting each flight an amount of fuel that I see fit, and I will base that amount on the length of time it *should* take you to complete the flight."

He then told us that he would be basing his figures on a clear day with still air, and he would not be taking winds and weather into account when he made his calculations. "The reason for this," he'd said, "is because, every time there's wind or snow or anything else, everybody ends up taking longer to get to their destination, and they try to blame the weather for their tardiness. This is a waste of fuel. So as of now there will be no more dilly dallying around and complaining that the winter weather, thunderstorms, or headwinds made you late, causing you to miss your deadlines and burn extra gas in the process. From now on, if you take too long to complete your flight, you are going to run out of gas. I doubt that any of you want that to happen, so I think that this is just the incentive that many of you need to be on time and more efficient."

Even upon request, he'd refused to give us any explanation as to how it could be possible to fly any faster or efficiently in the face of a strong headwind. "Just figure it out," he'd said.

So tonight, due to The Chief's new policy and the fifty-knot headwind we had encountered on the way to St. Louis, we were barely making it on fuel, and I was starting to get nervous.

The good news was, as we got closer to St. Louis, I was able to spot the airport. Sometimes, when the visibility is low as a result of fog, you will still be able to see the airport from the air. This is because the fog layer is so thin and close to the ground, that it becomes transparent when looking down through it. The problem was, once you got down low, such as during landing, you would descend into the fog layer and would now be looking through it long ways. At which point, visibility could drop to zero making it difficult to see the runway.

Landing in these conditions was completely illegal, but my options were limited. I could divert to a nearby alternate airport, one that was above minimums. The problem with that was; the courier wouldn't be there, he'd still be sitting at Park's waiting for us. After landing at the alternate airport, I'd have to call dispatch, to have them call the courier and send him to the airport we were at. It would definitely cause a huge delay, and deadlines would be missed.

The Chief had warned me that if I didn't complete this run to his satisfaction, he may decide to change his mind about letting me go on furlough. He knew I wanted out, and I actually think he would keep me around just as a punishment. I couldn't quit, because if I quit, I wouldn't qualify for unemployment. I had to laugh about this; *if I didn't do what The Chief considered to be a good job, I might not lose my job.* I knew what I had to do … I had to abandon air traffic control.

The control tower at the Parks Airport was closed this late at night, so the only person that could stand between us illegally landing there was the St. Louis approach controller I was currently in contact with. Normally, approach controllers won't pay attention to the weather at a secondary airport like Park's, unless they're specifically asked it. So, if I kept my mouth shut about the fog, and the controller didn't already know about it, maybe no one would ever know that we had landed below minimums. *Worth a shot*, I thought.

I reported to St. Louis Approach that I had the airport in sight and requested a visual approach*.

*- A Visual Approach allows pilots, who have the airport in sight, to proceed there by means of visual navigation. They may only be conducted under weather conditions that will allow the pilot to maintain the airport in sight throughout the approach. Our current situation, with the fog, would not, and was most definitely a disqualifier to legally conducting a visual approach. But, sometimes, ya gotta do what'cha gotta do.

"Checkflight 101, cleared for the visual into St. Louis Parks," the controller said.

"Checkflight 101 cleared for the visual," I read back.

This was good; he had cleared us for the visual. It meant that he had no idea what the weather at the airport was. If he had known about the fog, he would have advised me that the field was low IFR, and due to that, a visual approach would not be available.

"Checkflight 101 is ready to cancel IFR," I requested. This way we could continue to the airport on our own and no longer be in contact with air traffic control; this was just in case the controller happened to stumble upon a weather report within the next few minutes. If we were no longer in contact with him, it would be too late for him to tell us we couldn't land.

"Checkflight 101, IFR cancelation is received; radar service is terminated; frequency change is approved. See ya later," the controller said.

"See ya," I said, and we were on our own.

I switched the radio over to monitor the airport's advisory frequency. However, on the off chance that someone happened to be listening at the time, our arrival would be unannounced. I wasn't about to broadcast the fact that we were landing under these conditions. And, just for good measure, I decided to shut the transponder and all our lights off as well. Consequently, killing our radar signal and making us as invisible as possible.

I felt like we were about to pull a drive by on this airport. "We're in stealth mode, get your gat ready." I told The Co; a little reg breaking humor.

"Huh?" He didn't even look up from his game.

"Never mind."

I lined the plane up with the only runway that had an ILS approach, so I could use it to stay on the proper glide-path once we descended into the fog layer. The closer we got to the ground the dimmer the runway lights became. At about two hundred feet, upon actually entering the fog, the lights vanished. I held glideslope. For a few seconds it was pitch black. Then, at one-hundred feet the vague radiance of a couple white runway lights began to reappear. I still couldn't see the actual surface of the runway, just a few lights glowing on either side of me, but it was enough to know we were in the right place. I pulled the power to idle, held a slightly nose high pitch, and waited … Till … Thump. We touched down.

The Co looked up, "Damn it's dark here."

"Yeah, it's fog," I told him, as I slowed the plane.

We crept slowly down the runway, and I strained my eyes to find the taxiway.

"Where are we?" The Co asked. He was confused as usual.

"I think we're in St. Louis," I told him, "But I'm not sure yet, 'cause I can't see anything."

The Co sprung up in his seat. "Sweet, let's hit-up Sauget!"

"No. No time, it's just a quick stop."

I spotted the sign for Bravo two, "Hey, there's the taxiway!" I said, and made the turn.

The taxi to the ramp was slow through the murkiness, it was difficult to see anything.

"Hey, let's tell The Chief we're sick, so we can spend the night here and go to the strip clubs." The Co still wasn't giving up on that idea.

"No," I said. "You might be able to get away with faking sick, but not me. The Chief would never go for it. Besides, I really want to get home tonight." I still hadn't told him that this was my last night. I didn't want to jinx anything.

"Whatever, you're no fun." The Co said and slumped back down in his seat.

Eventually, we found our parking spot without hitting anything, and our serial killer-ish looking courier was there waiting. "Wanna help load," I asked The Co.

"Not if we can't go to Sauget."

"Yeah, that's what I figured."

I got out of the plane, only to be greeted by some god-awful evil noise (music) that blared from the courier's car. It sounded like the soundtrack to a lovely evening of eating babies. "Wow, did you just land in this fog?" The courier asked.

"No, we've been here." I told him, "We just taxied over from the other side of the ramp." There is no way he could have seen us land, and I'm not going to tell anyone anything incriminating, even if it was a brain-dead courier who had no idea what the regulations for landing minimums were.

"Who's this band?" I asked.

"Oh, it my band," he said excitedly, and then added, "You know, whenever you're in town for a while, you should check us out. We melt faces."

Melt faces, huh? They sounded like "The Cookie Monster Sings," if that album were ever to be made, and I'd rather go to Sauget with The Co.

But I told him, "Yeah … you guys sound good. Maybe next time—" And just when I needed an out, headlights appeared out of the fog and the fuel truck rolled up. "Hang on; I gotta go put my fuel order in," I said and left the courier to load the work on his own.

The fueler jumped down from his truck. "Hey man," he said. "Someone called from your company a few minutes ago and told me to only give you sixty-eight gallons of gas, exactly. Is that what you guys want?"

"Yeah," I said, "That was our chief pilot, that's all the fuel he'll allow us."

"Alright, I just thought it was sort of weird. I mean no one has ever called here before to put a limit on the amount of fuel for a flight."

"The company's broke."

"Ahh, I see. Well then, sixty-eight gallons it is."

"Thanks," I said, "thirty-four a side in the inboards."

"Got'cha," the fueler said, then he leaned in closer, "hey what's this music?"

"It's his band," I smirked and nodded towards the courier. "You should check them out, they melt faces."

"Pass."

"Same here," I assured him, and I went back to helping the cookie monster load the work.

Once the cargo was loaded up, I noticed that the fueler was struggling with the hose. I checked my watch and saw that we were already a couple minutes behind schedule. The headwinds on the way here combined with the slow taxi through the fog had slowed us down. We needed to get going like now if we were going to make the Chicago deadlines. "What's going on?" I asked the fueler.

"I don't know man, it just quit pumping."

"You've gotta be kidding me."

"No man, it's not pumping at all."

"Well how much did you get in there?" I was hoping to hear "all of it," though I knew that wouldn't be his answer.

"I got the thirty-four gallons in the left tank, then when I went to the right tank it wouldn't pump. I think I've gotta go get the spare fuel truck."

"Please hurry."

"Will do," he said and slowly drove off.

We were now going to be very late, and this was not the day to be late. For a second, I considered just going with the fuel we had, but we'd never make it to Chicago. Even with the whole sixty-eight gallons of allotted fuel, it would still be close. Making it on half that, would be impossible.

Several long impatient minutes passed till the fueler returned with the spare truck, and pumped the other thirty-four gallons in. When I started up the engines, once again I checked the time; it was late. *I'm screwed!* I thought, and I could just hear The Chief's disapproval, "You missed your Chicago deadlines. Guess you'll be with staying with us for a while." Not wanting that to happen, taxied across the ramp like a bandit, and despite the fact that I was blinded by the fog, we almost made it to the taxiway without hitting anything.

Just before the entrance to the taxiway, we clipped the left-wing tip on a parked airplane. At least that's what I think it was anyway. Thankfully the damage didn't sound too bad, so I pressed on.

As I made a tire screeching turn onto Taxiway Bravo, I called ATC, "Checkflight 101, on the ground at Park's, IFR to Midway." We were technically above takeoff minimums, that is if you consider The Co to be a qualified crew member, so this would be a legal departure.

"Checkflight 101, squawk 4621, you're released. Clearance is void in ten minutes; give me a call airborne," the controller said.

"Checkflight 101, squawking 4621, we'll give you a call airborne," I responded, and lowered my head for just a second to enter our squawk code into the transponder. That was all it took. I picked my head up to find that there were no longer any blue taxiway lights in view. All I could see was darkness. The airport lighting was on a timer at night, and it had just turned off.

"Oh shit!" I yelled, and quickly clicked my mic button to turn the lights back on. But it was too late; in my moment of blindness I had strayed towards the edge of the taxiway. When the lights came back on, the first one I saw was the one that our nose wheel crushed a half-second later. We dropped down into the grass somewhere between the taxiway and runway, but I had no idea exactly where. The plane thrashed about through the uneven landscape. I saw another blue taxiway light to the left then a white runway light on the right. It was chaos.

My only thought was; don't miss this deadline, and in what had to be the most reckless effort to stay on schedule that any freight dog has ever made, I slammed the throttles forward and hoped for the best.

"Should I pause my game?" The Co asked.

"Yes," I said, "and hang on!"

I might as well have been taking off with my eyes closed in the middle of an obstacle course. Other than the occasional random colored lights or taxiway signs, that we either hit or nearly hit, I couldn't see a thing. And we were accelerating into a black hole of varying terrain. One second it felt like we were on pavement, then the next we were bouncing through the grass. I just held the controls back, waited for the wheels to lift, and when they finally did; I put the gear up.

Upon breaking ground, it only took a few seconds until we were above the fog layer in clear skies. I contacted departure control. Next stop—Chicago.

An hour of monotonous cruise dragged by, there was nothing I could do to keep myself entertained. I just stared at my watch, and all I could think about was making this deadline and getting back to Ohio. The engines were running at weekend power, and thankfully the winds were a little more favorable on this leg. It was looking like an on-time arrival would still be possible, that is, unless we ran into any further delay. But the anticipation was killing me. Finally, I could make out the lights of Chicago, outlining the south shore of Lake Michigan in the distance.

Other than the occasional chatter of air traffic control it had been dead quite in the plane since we left St. Louis. Then, out of nowhere, The Co spoke. "Music," he said.

"Huh?" I questioned, figuring he was just having some sort of daydream or day-nightmare; who knows what's going on in his head. But then, I heard it.

For as long as I'd been a freight dog, there had been a mysterious

DJ of the night time sky. No one ever knew who it was, but at random times in the middle of the night, someone would broadcast music over our company frequency. It was always something ridiculous, but in comparison to the silent boredom up here in the middle of the night, any music was welcome. The week prior, we had been treated to, "I Will Always Love You," by Whitney Houston, while battling a thunderstorm near Louisville. It definitely wouldn't have been on my list of requests, but it was entertaining non-the-less.

Tonight's song choice was better though. In fact, I couldn't think of a more appropriate song for the moment; sort-of an ode to the back-side of the clock.

Well, my friends, the time has come
(To) raise the roof and have some fun
Throw away the work to be done
Let the music play on … (Play on, play, play on…)

The Co started drumming on his knees. "Turn it up, turn it up," he said impatiently. And I did. I cranked the volume so high that, had air traffic control tried to get a hold of us, I wouldn't have even been able to hear them. And for a moment, I didn't even care.

We're going to Party, Karamu, Fiesta, forever. Lionel Richie blasted into our headsets so loud that I couldn't even hear the engines backfiring anymore.

Come on and sing along!

"All night long! all night, all night All night Long!" I sang and The Co quickly joined me.

The two of us sang along at the top of our lungs, and though many may not be willing to admit to it, I bet that every other freight dog that was out there that night was singing along as well. All the tired old Navajo's, limping their way through the nighttime sky, for a few minutes at least, were flown by smiling singing pilots.

For me, it was sort of a sentimental moment. The last hurrah; the end of an era. As of tomorrow, I would no longer be a freight dog. I had no idea what lie ahead for me, most likely eight months of sitting on my couch, after which I'd have to get a job flipping burgers or something. But still, it felt great to know I was finally about to be free from the tyranny of Checkflight.

The Co got so jacked up that he slammed his Game Boy down and jumped on his seat. "Yeah, once you get started you can't sit down," he sang, "Come join the fun, it's a merry-go-round. Everyone's dancing their troubles away." He even flailed his arms about and bounced around the cockpit as he sang, "Come join our party, see how we play!" I think I may have even seen jazz fingers, it was out of control.

And then, just as The Co was pulling out his air trombone for the horn solo, abruptly, the song quit.

"Hey, what the hell," The Co said. "Who shut off the music?" He dropped back into his seat and crossed his arms. The fun was over.

Several long minutes of silence past; the music was gone. The Co picked up his Game Boy, and I went back to staring at my watch and worrying about the deadline. Once again, anxious boredom began to set in.

Then out of nowhere, over our same company frequency that the music had been playing on, somebody yelled, "Ramp Checks!" I have no idea who said it or where they were, but it didn't sound good.

The FAA randomly conducts ramp checks on pilots and aircraft to ensure they are being operated in compliance with the regulations. They can check anything they want on the airplane: paperwork, certificates, maintenance logs, etc.

Instantly, I forgot about the deadline, and my mood changed to panic. Something told me that whatever was going on tonight, in the wake of recent events, would not be your run-of-the-mill ramp check. I had a bad feeling that this might be something bigger.

I'd never been ramp checked before, so I really wasn't sure what to expect. I figured if I'd worked for a reputable airline, it would be a relatively pleasant, however slightly annoying experience; maybe similar to a routine traffic stop, where an FAA inspector would kindly ask to see my pilot's license and the required aircraft documents. "Yes sir, no problem," I'd say, and politely hand them over. But I didn't work for a reputable airline; I worked for Checkflight.

I'd always imagined that if I were ever to get ramp checked in one of Checkflight's airplanes, it would probably more closely resemble the finale to a high-speed police chase. I could just picture The Co and I being dragged out of the Navajo, thrown facedown onto the tarmac, and cuffed at gun point. *Or maybe it'd go down like a swat team raid*, I thought; where FAA Inspectors donning riot gear, would kick the windows in on our airplane and shove assault rifles in our faces while demanding to see our certificates.

I was starting to get nervous. Even if you disregard everything that had just happened in St. Louis, nothing about this flight or this airplane was anywhere near being in compliance. Checkflight's airplanes never were, and the list of items the Feds could ding us on was endless.

The Navajo we were flying had a bit of an oil leak, and, when I say a bit of an oil leak, I mean that it had a severe oil leak that was consuming several quarts a day. If they put all of our cargo on a scale, it would not match the numbers on our paperwork. Not even close, because nothing at Checkflight was ever weighed. The numbers on our paperwork were just eyeballed estimates. Our left-wing tip was smashed from the plane we'd clipped in St. Louis. And thanks to The

Chiefs new fuel limitations, once again we'd be landing on fumes. We wouldn't even be in the ballpark of having the legally required amount of reserve fuel. And if that wasn't enough, I could go on.

Then I thought about The Co. He probably had alcohol in system, possibly other drugs as well, and was most likely in possession. "You got anything illegal on you?" I asked him. "Alcohol? drugs?"

The Co stared at me as if I was an idiot. "Alcohol is not illegal," he said.

"It is when you're flying an airplane."

"Really? I thought it was just frowned upon." It was obvious that this was news to him.

"No, it's definitely illegal."

"Well in that case, then yes I've got some whiskey—" he hesitated as if there were more.

"And?"

"And a couple joints," he confessed.

"Fork it over."

"Why?"

"'Cause, I think some shit's about to go down."

"Fine, but you owe me," he said, and began digging in his bag.

He handed me a sandwich bag that had two joints in it and a fifth of whiskey that was half-empty. "What are you going to do with it?" he asked.

"I'm throwing all of it out the storm window."

"Really?"

"Yes," I said, and I opened the window and let the bag of weed go. Then I shoved the whiskey bottle out; it shattered when it hit the tail.

"If anything happens when we land in Chicago, just stay quiet and let me do the talking." I told him.

"Yeah, whatever," The Co mumbled.

I was still in a hurry to make the deadline, just in case this was all a false alarm. That's what I was hoping for anyway. Upon request, Midway Tower cleared us to make a straight-in landing on runway four-right, which gave us the shortest distance between us and the ramp. I touched-down as close to the beginning of the runway as possible, got on the brakes hard, and made the first right turnoff towards the ramp.

"Remember, if anyone starts asking questions, just stay quiet," I reminded The Co as I rounded the corner onto the ramp.

And that's when I saw him. My heart stopped.

There was a guy in a suit standing on the ramp right in our parking spot. No one in a suit is ever out here at this time of night. It had to be a Fed.

This was it, I thought. *It's over.*

A wave of panic rushed over me and my first instinct was to set the plane on fire and run for the fence. I told myself, if you get caught, deny everything; claim you've never seen that plane before in your life. And that's just what we did.

I hit the brakes, stopping the plane about fifty yards from where the fed was standing, and killed the engines. "Get ready to run," I said to The Co.

The Co looked at me confused, and asked, "Why?"

"Just follow me!" I fumbled in my flight bag and pulled out a lighter, then tore a page out of the maintenance log. "Let's go!" I flung the side door open and jumped out onto the wing. The Co nonchalantly climbed over my seat towards the door.

"Hurry!" I said. "It's a bust!"

As soon as I said "bust," I got The Co's attention, apparently that was a word he was familiar with. He quickly followed me as I jumped off the wing and ran towards the fuel caps on right side of the plane. I lit the maintenance log page and opened the fuel cap.

That's when I heard, "Hey stop right there!" We had caught the FAA inspector by surprise, and it took him a second to realize what was happening, but as soon as he saw the flaming paper in my hand, he came sprinting towards us.

Without hesitation, I tossed the burning paper in the fuel tank.

"Go!" I screamed. "Run for the fence!"

The Navajo erupted in flames behind us and The Co and I ran like our lives depended on it. Within seconds, police cars and just about every vehicle that could have possibly been on the airport appeared out of the woodwork. They were all speeding in our direction, lights flashing and sirens wailing.

They had been waiting for us.

The Co and I reached the brick fence that surrounded Midway Airport. I looked back at our burning Navajo and the swarm of law enforcement screaming towards us. It was a surreal scene, but somehow, this is how I'd always known it would end.

"I'll give you a boost on top of the wall, then you pull me up." I told The Co, and lifted him up by his feet.

The Co gripped the ledge, and pulled himself up on the wall. "Grab my arm.," he said, and reached down for my hand. Our Navajo exploded behind us, as I jumped and locked onto his hand.

He started to hoist me up. But suddenly, something hit me in the back. I was stricken by debilitating pain, and lost my grip.

I fell to the ground, and looked up to see the cop who had just shot me in the back with a taser, along with several other people who were bearing down on us.

"Come on, get up!" The Co said.

I tried to stand but, I couldn't. My whole body was numb.

"Come on!" The Co yelled again.

I was paralyzed. "Run!" I told him, "I can't move."

I could feel stomping footsteps all around.

I looked up at The Co and saw a taser dart wiz right by him, missing by just inches. He still stood there with his arm outstretched, and again yelled, "Get up!"

I wasn't going to make it. And somehow, I knew this would be the last time I saw The Co. All I could think to say was, "It's been ... real."

The Co saw my defeat, "Peace out," he said, and he jumped down off the other side of the wall.

A few hours later, in the Fed's office, they filled me in on the status of my coworkers. Checkflight's motor home headquarters had been raided like it was a meth lab. SWAT teams had burst through the windows with assault rifles, tearing the place apart. Even Barbara had been cuffed and dragged off.

While that was happening, FAA inspectors had been waiting for our flights at airports all over the country. Every plane in the fleet was stopped on the ground for a ramp check, and all of the pilots had been taken into custody.

The Feds knew everything, and there was an endless list of violations against the employees of Checkflight. Some were simple, such as, one pilot who was being charged with sixteen violations, which included: unsecured cargo, numerous maintenance discrepancies, incomplete paperwork, and it was questionable whether the airworthiness certificate for his airplane was valid, but that would require further investigation. Others were charged with more serious offenses, such as; drug trafficking, money laundering, and one that was news to me: coyote crossing.

The Chief had been operating a taxi for illegal immigrants down in Texas, piling as many as twenty people in the back of a Navajo on each flight.

"Then another was busted using his dog in lieu of a required crewmember." The inspector told me.

"What?" I asked.

"Yeah, we couldn't hardly believe it ourselves." The inspector said. "The guy had his dog strapped into the right seat. Claimed the dog was trained to bark callouts."

"Huh? A real freight dog."

The inspector continued to carry on for several minutes with his list of charges that were being brought against the pilots of Checkflight.

"What about The Chief?" I interrupted. "He's the one behind all this."

The inspector then told me that The Chief's motor home bedroom\office was raided during the bust. "He tried to make a run for it," The inspector said, "by attempting a getaway in a stolen Piper Tri-Pacer, which has a top speed of sixty knots. Within minutes he was intercepted by F-16s who advised to him to land. He didn't go down without a fight though. They had to fire a few warning shots over his wings, just to let him know they were serious. After that, he changed his attitude about running, and promptly landed at the nearest airport. We have him in custody." The inspector then shook his head when he told me, "The list of evidence we found against The Chief when we went through his office is so long, I don't even know where to begin. But by far the most disturbing thing we found was that there was a pilot employed at Checkflight who didn't even have a pilot's license."

"What?"

"Yeah, The Chief hired a pilot two years ago without ever checking his pilot's certificates," the inspector said. "You may know him as The Co."

"Well, that explains a lot," I said, and I was reminded of The Co being touted as a model employee. He wasn't even a pilot.

The inspector then told me that The Chief had already admitted that he'd discovered that The Co was not a pilot about a year ago. He had even confronted The Co about it.

"I didn't know I needed a pilot's license," The Co had said.

"But why would you apply for a pilot job if you didn't even know how to fly?" The Chief had asked.

"I just needed a job," The Co had said. "I applied for a lot of jobs. I applied for a position as a surgeon too, but they didn't hire me; you did."

"Well," The Chief had said, "you've been working here for a year already; it's too late to fix this now. Just do as I say and don't tell anybody that you're not really a pilot, and I won't either."

"The Chief is going to be locked up for a long time," the inspector told me, "and we're still trying to track down this guy called The Co."

"So, what about me?" I asked.

"Well," the inspector said, "let's take a look at your file."

Alex Stone

- 12 -
The Aftermath

The Co doesn't fly anymore. No other airline would ever hire him since it was discovered that he was never a pilot in the first place.

He now lives under the 16th Street Bridge and goes by the name Alphonso Tremayne Rodríguez-Dejuan IV. He was last seen drinking a warm six-pack of Schlitz.

Chip was never seen or heard from again. A few weeks after stealing the airplane and crew car, his ex-wife's new lover's HALO character was found dead. The stolen crew car was found wrapped around a tree outside Pensacola.

Phillip the Miniature Dachshund (Chip's second ex-wife's ex-dog) made it to New York City and invested the twenty-dollar bill that had been pinned to his collar on Wall Street, earning him billions. He is now the CEO of a major investment firm that currently runs on government TARP money. He is still not housebroken and regularly shits in his office.

Vladimir the courier from Omaha became a mini-celebrity around Checkflight after I showed everyone the picture I had taken of him. All the pilots started to fight over any flight that went to Omaha, so they could get a chance to meet him in person.

When Checkflight collapsed, he reportedly got a paper route delivering The Omaha Daily News. He wakes up early every morning to deliver the paper in his mini-van while wearing his pinstripe suit.

Tony the Mechanic is now a customer service representative for a major PC software company. He spends his days trying to convince disgruntled customers that the software works fine, "you just don't know how to use it." And if they disagree, he threatens them with a shanking.

Sherman (Karen's maybe husband) is real after all. He is not, however, in the army, a pilot, an ultimate cage fighting champion, or a congressman. He is a security guard at their apartment complex earning five dollars a day to watch the shed and make sure none of the lawn mowers are stolen.

Karen the Dispatcher is now a hairdresser. She spends her days bragging to her clients about everything she wishes Sherman could be.

Barbara the Dispatcher still shows up for work daily even after repeatedly being told that the company is no longer in business. Every day she sits at her desk, which the airport authority has allowed her to keep in an abandoned hangar, and waits for the phone to ring. The phone is no longer connected to a line, but, because her memory is fading, she is no longer aware that it hasn't rang in months. Upon being reminded that the airline had shut down and she could go home she replied, "THE CHICKENS ARE LOOSE!"

Rick moved back to his hometown of Atlanta. He is now off the juice and lives a happily sleeveless life running his own landscaping business; "Sans Sleeves Landscaping of Georgia."

Rick's copilot later realized that their stunt in Chicago nearly cost them their lives. He claims that he has found Jesus, and he now runs a successful televangical program that airs on Sunday mornings at four a.m.

The Chief now awaits federal trial on several hundred counts of Federal Aviation Regulation violations.

As for me… By agreeing to testify against The Chief, I was able to cop a plea deal, which included; unemployment benefits, and only a temporary suspension of my pilot's license. My license has recently been reinstated, and I am still looking for another job in aviation.

Read the prequel to *Hauling Checks,*
CFI! The Book,
now available in paperback and on Kindle

Alex Stone

About the Author:

Alex Stone grew up in Munster, Indiana. He's been flying since age fourteen and received a Bachelor's Degree in Aviation Science from Western Michigan University. He has worked as a flight instructor and was a "Freight Dog" in the air cargo industry for seven years. *Hauling Checks* is his first novel. In 2018 he published his second novel *CFI! The Book*.

Alex Stone

Glossary of Aviation Terms

AIR ROUTE TRAFFIC CONTROL CENTER (ARTCC) or "CENTER" - A facility established to provide air traffic control service to aircraft operating on IFR flight plans within controlled airspace and principally during the en route phase of flight.

AIR TRAFFIC CONTROL (ATC) - A service operated by the appropriate authority to promote the safe, orderly, and expeditious flow of air traffic.

BRAKING ACTION - A report of conditions on the airport movement area providing a pilot with a degree/quality of braking that he/she might expect. Braking action is reported in terms of good fair, poor, or nil.

CEILING - The heights above the earth's surface of the lowest layer of clouds or obscuring phenomena that is reported as "broken," "overcast," or "obscuration," and not classified as "thin" or "partial."

CLEARANCE - Authorization given by ATC to proceed as requested or instructed (for example: "Cleared for takeoff," "Cleared for visual approach," or "Cleared to land").

CLEARANCE DELIVERY - Control tower position responsible for transmitting departure clearances to IFR flights.

COMMON TRAFFIC "ADVISORY FREQUENCY" (CTAF) - A frequency designed for the purpose of carrying out airport advisory practices while operating to or from an airport without an operating control tower.

CONSTANT SPEED PROPELLER - A controllable pitch propeller, whose pitch is automatically varied in flight by a prop-governor to maintain a constant preselected r.p.m., in spite of varying air loads.

CONTROL TOWER or "TOWER" - A terminal facility that uses air/ground communications, visual signaling, and other devices to provide ATC services to aircraft operating in the vicinity of an airport or on the movement area. Authorizes aircraft to land or take off at the airport controlled by the tower.

COWLING - A circular, removable fairing around an aircraft engine for the purposes of streamlining or cooling.

DECISION HEIGHT (DH) - A specified height in the precision approach at which a missed approach must be initiated if the required visual reference to continue the approach has not been established.

DE-ICE BOOTS or "BOOTS" - A device installed on aircraft surfaces to permit mechanical de-icing in flight. Consists of a thick rubber membrane that is installed over the surface. As atmospheric icing occurs and ice builds up, a pneumatic system inflates the boot with compressed air. This expansion cracks any ice that has accumulated, and this ice is then blown away by the airflow. The boots are then deflated to return the wing or surface to its optimal shape.

FEDERAL AVIATION ADMINISTRATION (FAA) or "FEDS" - Organization in charge of defining the aviation safety standards in the USA.

FIXED BASE OPERATOR (FBO) - A commercial operator supplying fuel, maintenance, flight training, and other services at an airport.

FINAL APPROACH or "FINAL" - One of the many words describing the approach segments. The part of a landing sequence or aerodrome circuit procedure in which the aircraft has made its final turn and is inbound to the active runway.

FLIGHT PLAN - Specified information relating to the intended flight of an aircraft, filed orally or in writing with a Flight Service

Station or an Air Traffic Control facility.

FLIGHT SERVICE STATION (FSS) - Air traffic facilities which provide pilot briefing, en route communications and VFR search and rescue services, assist lost aircraft and aircraft in emergency situations, relay ATC clearances, originate Notices to Airmen, broadcast aviation weather and NAS information, receive and process IFR flight plans, and monitor NAVAIDs. In addition, at selected locations, FSSs provide Enroute Flight Advisory Service (Flight Watch), take weather observations, issue airport advisories, and advise Customs and Immigration of transborder flights.

GLIDE SLOPE or "GLIDE PATH" - A tightly focused radio beam transmitted from the approach end of a runway indicating the minimum approach angle that will clear all obstacles; one component of an instrument landing system (ILS).

GROUND CONTROL or "GROUND" - Tower control, by radioed instructions from air traffic control, of aircraft ground movements at an airport.

INSTRUMENT APPROACH – A series of predetermined maneuvers for the orderly transfer of an aircraft under instrument flight conditions from the beginning of the initial approach to a landing, or to a point from which a landing may be made visually.

INSTRUMENT LANDING SYSTEM (ILS) - A radar-based system allowing ILS-equipped aircraft to find a runway and land when clouds may be as low as 200' (or lower for special circumstances).

LOCALIZER – A tightly focused radio beam transmitted from the approach end of a runway indicating lateral deviations from a preset course; one component of an instrument landing system (ILS).

MAGNETO – An accessory that produces and distributes a high-voltage electric current for ignition of a fuel charge in an internal combustion engine.

PILOT IN COMMAND (PIC) - The pilot responsible for the operation and safety of an aircraft during flight time.

RUNWAY VISUAL RANGE (RVR) or "VISABILITY" - A horizontal measurement of visibility along a runway.

STALL - Sudden loss of lift when the angle of attack increases to a point where the flow of air breaks away from a wing or airfoil, causing it to drop.

TRANSPONDER – An airborne transmitter that responds to ground-based interrogation signals to provide air traffic controllers with more accurate and reliable position information than would be possible with "passive" radar; may also provide air traffic control with an aircraft's altitude.

VECTOR – Compass heading instructions issued by ATC in providing navigational guidance by radar.

VISUAL APPROACH or "VISUAL" – An approach conducted on an IFR flight plan that authorizes the pilot to proceed visually and clear of clouds to the airport.

www.haulingchecks.com

Also by Alex Stone:

CFI! The Book

An underpaid, overworked Certified Flight Instructor cheats death while attempting to teach a cast of incompetent student pilots to fly at a skeezy South Florida flight school; all in the quest to build flight time so he can get a "real job" at an airline. The planes break, the regs break, metal gets bent, students are lost at sea, and a Top Gun wannabe student, who has four hundred hours of flight instruction, still hasn't made his first solo flight. "CFI! The Book" is an over-the-top satirical aviation comedy that's loosely based on real world experiences of flight instruction, but if the FAA asks, this is all strictly fictional.

ISBN 13: 978-1790668793

Fiction / Transportation / Aviation / Flight Instruction

Fiction / Humorous / Satire

Paperback, 5.25x8, 154pp; Kindle (.mobi)

BUY *CFI! THE BOOK* ON AMAZON

Available in paperback or on Kindle

www.cfithebook.com

Made in the USA
Columbia, SC
01 March 2021